Ann Hammerton was brought up in Nottingham where her parents ran successful companies. After an eventful life in theatre, commerce and property renovation in the UK and abroad, she now lives in Eastbourne where she continues to work on ideas for future novels.

DOUBLE DOUBT

the story of an obsession

Ann Hammerton

DOUBLE DOUBT

the story of an obsession

AUSTIN & MACAULEY
PUBLISHERS LTD.

A CIP catalogue record for this title is
available from the British Library.

ISBN 978 1 84963 194 5

www.austinmacauley.com

First Published (2012)
Austin & Macauley Publishers Ltd.
25 Canada Square
Canary Wharf
London
E14 5LB

Printed & Bound in Great Britain

This story is dedicated to all those who long to find their roots, and to separated twins everywhere.

CHAPTER ONE

London 1990

Judy Hay arrived at the tube station a bit later than usual that morning. The train came in crowded, but not unbearably so. She jumped on and grabbed the metal bar by the opposite door.

At the next stop a tall, good-looking man got on, followed by a woman in a red coat, pushed towards him by the following commuters. The man was trying to read a newspaper which he was holding with one hand, while he hung on to a hanging roof strap with the other. Judy had a feeling that he and the woman were together, although he stood with his back to her as though unaware of her presence. She wondered if they were one of those couples who don't talk to each other in the morning, or if perhaps they had had a row over breakfast.

Judy pushed her thoughts to the busy day ahead, when, glancing up, she saw the woman place a hand over the man's holding on to the hanging strap. He shook it off angrily, muttering something without even turning his head. I was right, thought Judy; they've obviously had a row.

Looking again at the red-coated woman, she became aware of a strange feeling of familiarity, even affinity. It looks like the back of me in my red coat standing there.

She shivered, glancing again towards the woman.

She was about the same height and build as Judy, and her hair too was ash-blonde. She couldn't see her face, or even her profile, but she could have been about the same age. Then, glancing down, Judy noticed that she was wearing low-heeled black shoes almost identical to her own! Who on earth is she?

Judy stared as the newspaper held by the man began to shake. He muttered something turning sharply to face the woman. The train slowed down and ran into the next station and, as the door opened, the woman in red leaped out and started down the platform. Judy looked up and gasped as she caught a glimpse of the woman's face through the carriage window. It was as though she was looking at her own reflection in a mirror!

"Bloody Hell," she muttered. "I've got a double!" Then, balancing on her toes, she strained to look over the heads of the passengers in front of her, scanning the platform as the train moved off again. But the woman in the red coat had disappeared. *I must find out who she is,* she thought, then, remembering that she had got on at Pimlico and left at Victoria, she decided to look out for her the next day.

The tall man's newspaper fell to the floor, and as Judy bent down to retrieve it, his hand slipped from the overhead strap, hitting her sharply on the head.

"Hey! Do you mind…" her protest fading as the man crumpled and fell to the floor, his head landing on her foot.

"Quick someone… help! This man's fainted." Some of the people nearby cleared a space around the fallen man.

A young Indian man pushed his way forward. "Let

me through. I'm a doctor," he pleaded. As he knelt down, Judy moved her foot, causing the man's head to slide heavily to the floor. His eyes were wide open. Judy crouched down to take his hand, their eyes met; a hoarse whisper came from the back of his throat.

"Suzi… No!" Then his head rolled back, his mouth still open.

"There's no pulse," muttered the young Indian doctor, his hand against the man's neck, and kneeling up, thumped hard on the man's breastbone with his fist.

"Oh God! He's not going to die, is he?" asked a horrified Judy.

"He's had a heart attack!" announced a woman nearby. "Someone had better call an ambulance."

"Let me through," urged a large man wearing a black leather jacket over well-worn jeans. "Somebody stop the train… pull the red emergency handle by the door," he ordered, taking charge. "How's he doing?" he asked the doctor. The young Indian shook his head.

"It doesn't look good."

"Here, let me take over. It's all right, I'm with the police. You call the hospital, doctor."

The train's brakes screamed as it shuddered to a halt.

"What's going on? We'll be late for work," complained a man further down the carriage, while the policeman continued pummelling the unconscious man's chest.

"It's nearly five minutes," said the doctor.

"All right, you take it now," said the policeman, as he stood up to retrieve his mobile phone. The next station was alerted and the train moved slowly off again.

"There'll be an ambulance waiting," the policeman told the doctor some minutes later, "but I should stop now if I were you. This man is dead." The young Indian continued pumping for a few more minutes, unwilling to give up hope, then, with tears in his eyes, he stood up and turned away, shaking his head in despair.

Judy too felt her eyes misting over. It was such a shock. Only minutes ago there was this super-looking man standing next to her, and now he was lying dead at her feet.

"Look!" she cried, pointing to the floor. A spreading puddle of blood was seeping out from the side of his body. The policeman knelt down for a closer look.

"This man has a knife wound. Ladies and gentlemen!" he called in a loud voice. "As there has been an unfortunate incident in the carriage, there will be a slight delay, and I cannot allow anyone to leave the station just yet."

"For God's sake man, we have to get to work! I've got an important meeting at nine o'clock," yelled one smartly-dressed man.

"And I'll get the sack if I'm late again," moaned a young girl. The hundred or so people in the carriage joined in the general commotion, while some yelled frantically into their mobile phones, as the train pulled in to the next station.

The carriage doors slid open to reveal a group of uniformed policemen headed by a senior looking officer.

"Come along now, this won't take long, ladies and gentlemen; this way please," he ordered, as he led the travellers out of the train.

"Come with me, doctor," said the plain-clothed policeman to the young Indian. "We will need your statement first, and you too, madam," he added, turning to Judy.

As Judy followed them into the station, she glanced back to see two white-coated men enter the carriage to examine the body, and she felt suddenly sick. Had the doctor noticed that the man had mistaken her for the woman in the red coat? And had she really killed the man? THE WOMAN WHO LOOKED EXACTLY LIKE HER?

When Judy reached the station, she was dismayed to see that it was the policeman who had been there who was to question her, and she knew, in that instance, that she wasn't going to tell him what she had seen. I know her... she's part of my past, I'm sure, and I won't tell the police the name she whispered.

"You were standing right next to the man weren't you?" asked the policeman.

"Well yes, you know I was," she replied.

"Did you know this man?"

"No, I've never seen him before."

"You've never seen him before on the tube in the morning?"

"No, never," said Judy, wondering, now what?

"Did you notice if there was anyone with him?"

"No, I'm pretty sure he was alone," she replied carefully.

"Or if there was anyone perhaps jostling him?"

"There were people pushing to get on behind him, so in the circumstances, I don't see how anyone could have seen what happened. Like everyone else, I was just trying to avoid getting crushed."

"Fair enough," said the policeman smiling. "Just leave me your name and address, Miss, and if we need any further information we will contact you over the next few days." Judy stood up to leave.

"You do realize that you may have witnessed a crime?"

"Yes; but as I have said, I really don't think that I can be of much help. May I go now?"

"Of course," he replied smiling. "Have a good day, Miss Hay!"

"Is that supposed to be funny?" she muttered as she left.

Judy's boss was sitting at her desk, checking through his diary when she arrived at the offices of the Kuwaiti-owned trading company where she worked.

"I'm sorry I'm late, John," she apologised, as he stood up to greet her.

"No problem, Jude, but you do look a bit frazzled; are you not feeling too good?"

"I'm all right, at least I think I am. We got held up at the station by the police."

"The police? What's happened? Not another bomb?"

"No, thank God, but the man standing next to me on the tube dropped dead. Somebody stabbed him."

"Good God, Ducky!" exclaimed John. "That's terrible! No wonder you look upset."

"Yes I suppose I am. It must be the shock."

"Did you see what happened?"

"No, not really, but I have a good idea."

"Do you mean you think you know who did it?" asked John, incredulous.

"Yes, and that's what makes it so frightening."

"It surely wasn't someone you know, Judy?"

"Oh no... at least, I don't think so," she mumbled, turning away from his puzzled gaze.

"My dear girl, whatever do you mean?" John walked

over to place his arms around her.

Judy had been John's assistant for five years, and during that time they had become close friends.

A good twenty-five years older than Judy, John was a cross between a conspiratorial brother and a protective father.

"I shouldn't have told you that," she said, looking up at him. "Please John, promise me you won't mention what I said to anyone else?"

"But Judy, you could be in danger if you were a witness! Surely you told the police?"

"I told them that I couldn't help them, John, and I can't."

"But that's ridiculous, you must tell them everything you saw. If you witnessed a murder they should protect you."

"It's more complicated than that," she admitted. "I can't tell the police... not yet."

"Well my dear, I just hope you know what you are doing. Whatever it is that is worrying you, you know you can count on me, but for heaven's sake, Ducky, any sign of trouble – you call the police, because if you don't, then I will!"

"Oh John, you are so good. I shouldn't have told you, but what I saw was so incredible, and frightening in the circumstances, that I need some time to think about it. It wasn't just that a man was killed next to me, John, there was something else. But it'll be all right, really. Now I'd better get on with some work, otherwise you'll be giving me the sack."

"Silly girl! Just get me McDermott on the phone, will you? Then we'd better have some coffee."

CHAPTER TWO

Suzanne rushed down the platform at Victoria, her heart pounding against her ribs. She hardly knew where she was going as she stumbled and pushed her way through the commuters towards the stairs leading up to the main station. Beads of sweat and tears started to drip down her face; she felt hot and struggled to breathe.

"You bastard, Graham!" she muttered. "You made me do it!" Pausing for a moment, she unbuttoned her overcoat and, as she threw it over her arm, she tripped and fell heavily against the central stair guard rail.

"Shite!" she screamed, as a young man grabbed hold of her arm.

"Are you all right?" he asked, staring shocked at the deranged young woman.

"Oh, just leave me alone!" she yelled, pushing him out of the way to make a dash for the top of the stairs.

"What's up with her? She looks terrible," he remarked to his companion.

As Suzanne reached the station concourse, her head began to clear. She knew she had to get away from there quickly, but how could she get back to the flat? There was a long queue at the taxi rank, and to wait for a bus would be crazy. She would have to walk.

Minutes later, hurrying along Grosvenor Crescent, Suzanne spotted a bus going up to Marble Arch and jumped on. She found a seat near the front and sat hunched up, her eyes closed tight. The bus was halfway down Park Lane before she began to be aware of the enormity of what she had done. Her shaking hands clutched the handbag which still held the knife she had plunged into Graham. She was sure that no one had seen her do it, yet she sensed that somebody had been watching her when she left the train. She sat up suddenly, her heart beating wildly as she saw again the startled face of a woman staring at her through the train window. Shite! She looked familiar. And what had she seen? She began to shake all over and, as she moved her legs to one side to allow the woman next to her to pass, her bag fell heavily to the floor.

"Give it to me!" she snapped at the astonished woman who had bent to retrieve it.

"Oh, I'm sorry; I was just trying to help," stammered the embarrassed woman before fleeing to the exit.

Georgie was in the kitchen when Suzanne walked, breathless into the flat. "Is that you, Su?" she called. "I thought you'd gone for the day. God! What's happened to you, and where's your coat?" she asked, turning to notice Suzanne's agitation. "Are you all right, Su? You've been crying. You haven't seen that bastard boyfriend, have you?"

Suzanne flopped down onto a chair, her head in her hands. "I think I've killed him," she announced.

"What? What are you talking about?" yelled Georgie, grabbing hold of her friend's hands. Suzanne's body started to heave with racking sobs.

"Not Graham? You haven't seen him, have you?" Georgie was on her knees, shaking Suzanne as if to bring her to her senses.

"I never meant to hurt him, I love him, but why did he do it? Why to me, of all people? He loved me, I know he did. I don't know what to do." Georgie grabbed Suzanne and pulled her to her feet.

"Help me!" sobbed Suzanne.

"Look at me, Su," ordered her friend. "For God's sake stop crying, and tell me what's happened. What have you done?"

CHAPTER THREE

That evening Judy caught the tube home as usual, but when the train doors opened at Victoria, she found herself straining to catch sight of the woman in the red coat.

Oh how silly, she thought. If she really had stabbed that man, she would hardly be likely to be on the train tonight. But she couldn't help herself as she continued to scan the people around her. Perhaps it wasn't her; it could just as easily have been someone else. Was she perhaps trying to defend the woman because she was an image of herself in order to alleviate her fear of being suspected? Or could there be some remote possibility that she did have an identical twin sister? Judy sat up with a start. Now I really am being ridiculous, she chided herself.

The train stopped at Pimlico and, pushing her thoughts to one side, Judy opened up her 'freebie' newspaper and started to read.

"Good evening, Miss Hay!" Startled, she looked up. It was the policeman who had been on the train that morning.

"Good evening, Officer! You haven't been here all day, have you?" He laughed as he sat on the empty seat beside her.

"My name is Jones, Detective Sergeant Jones," he said, introducing himself, "and no, I haven't been here all day; just since four thirty."

Well, at least he seems friendly. Maybe I'm not a suspect – not yet anyway, thought Judy.

"Have you had any luck yet with witnesses?"

"No so far. It looks like it'll take some time, but in the meantime, Miss Hay, as you were standing next to the victim, I would like to have another chat with you."

Oh Lord, here we go! thought Judy.

"All right Sergeant Jones, but I've told you all I know," she lied. "And I don't really think there is anything else."

"I'll come with you, if you don't mind," said the policeman, as Judy stood up to leave the train at Stockwell.

Oh Lord!

"Of course; but I'm afraid you'll be wasting your time."

As they walked the few hundred yards to Judy's block of flats, her mind began to race. Should she tell him about the woman in the red coat? Because if she didn't and he had seen her standing on the other side of the man, he would be pretty sure she was lying. But whatever happened, there was no way she was going to tell anyone that she had been mistaken for the woman, and knew her name!

By the time they had reached the door to Judy's flat, she knew what she would say. "Do sit down, Sergeant, I'm dying for a cup of tea; would you like one?"

"That would be very welcome, Miss Hay." He placed his jacket over the back of a chair and took out his notebook. Judy handed him a mug of strong tea and sat down on the sofa opposite him.

"Now, Miss Hay. Can we go over everything you saw this morning, from when the victim got on at Pimlico until he fell to the floor."

Judy sighed and took a deep breath. "Well, as you know, Sergeant…"

"Detective Sergeant, if you don't mind, Miss," he interrupted. Judy winced.

"As you know, Detective Sergeant Jones, I got on the tube at Stockwell. The carriage was already crowded and I had to stand. When the man got on at Pimlico, I was standing on the opposite side, and he was being pushed towards me. He was trying to read a newspaper, which I thought was rather ridiculous."

"Yes, go on. Tell me about the other people who got on behind him."

"Oh gosh! I really didn't take much notice of them, apart from the fact that they were pushing and shoving to get on."

"You were standing on one side of him, weren't you? Now think, who did you see standing near him?"

"I'm sorry, I really can't remember," lied Judy, blushing. "I was amused watching him trying to read his squashed-up newspaper; I don't think I looked at the other people. But when he dropped his paper, and I bent down to pick it up, his hand hit me on the head!"

"Eh? You didn't tell me that this morning. Was that when he fell down?"

"Yes, it was just after Victoria."

"Why did he hit you? Was he holding his hand up in the air, or signalling at someone perhaps?"

"No." Judy smiled. "He was holding onto one of the overhead straps and, as he collapsed, his hand slid out and caught me as I stood up with his paper!"

"And what happened to the newspaper?"

"I don't know, it's probably still on the train."

"Now, Miss Hay," continued the policeman. "Are you absolutely sure you didn't notice anyone near to him when he fell? I find it difficult to believe that you didn't at least glance up when it happened."

"Perhaps I did," said Judy, "but I really don't remember. I just yelled for help. I was only aware of this poor man lying collapsed on the floor."

"All right. Let me just ask you this: a lot of the passengers must have got off at Victoria. Did you not look up and notice anything particular about any of them?"

Oh God, this is it, thought Judy. *He's going to ask me about the woman in the red coat.*

Judy swallowed the last of her tea and placed her mug down on a side table. "Yes, of course I saw people get off, but I didn't notice anything specific." Oh Lord, now he's made me lie again. The policeman was by now looking searchingly at Judy.

"I have statements from two passengers, Miss Hay, that there was a woman wearing a red coat who jumped off at Victoria and seemed to be in a hurry. Did you not notice a woman in a red coat, Miss Hay, or where she was standing?"

"Oh Hell, Sergeant! I mean, Detective Sergeant; look; I really don't remember noticing anyone in particular."

"Don't you think that a woman in a red coat would stand out on a crowded tube train?"

"Perhaps so." Judy's heart was pounding. "But as I have already said, all that I was aware of was the poor man lying on the floor."

"All right, Miss Hay," said Jones, snapping his notebook shut. "I think that will do for today. If you can drag anything else up from your memory, you will please give me a call, won't you?"

"Of course," replied Judy. "I'm sorry I couldn't be of much help. I suppose I am considered as a suspect as I was so near to the man."

"All the passengers in the carriage will be treated as suspects, Miss Hay, until we can come up with some concrete evidence, so I hope you are not thinking of popping off on holiday or anything, are you?"

"No, I'm not going anywhere; I shall be working right up to Christmas."

"Thank you, Miss Hay," said Jones, as he rose to leave. "Good evening."

"Thank goodness that's over," muttered Judy, as she closed the door behind the policeman. She carried the tea mugs into the kitchen and poured herself a large glass of wine, determined to blot out the memory of the dead man at her feet. She sat down on the sofa but, as she raised the glass to her mouth, she saw again the image of the woman in red as she hurried along the platform at Victoria. She had only seen a part of her face through the carriage window, but she knew without any doubt that the woman was her exact double. It wasn't only her face, but the way she held her head; and too, the way she stood on the tube, leaning slightly on one hip, just as Judy knew that she did. Then there were her shoes, and even her coat was similar to Judy's red one.

This is ridiculous, she told herself. I can't possibly have a twin. I was an only child, and I couldn't have been adopted, because I know mummy and daddy would have told me. So who on earth can she be, and why does she look just like me? Judy's head started to fill with all sorts of weird explanations until she finally decided to have a talk with her mother when she went to see her at the weekend.

CHAPTER FOUR

The phone rang, startling Judy as she stepped out of the shower. She stumbled into the bedroom and grabbed the receiver, hesitating for a moment before answering.

"Hello, Gorgeous, I'm back!"

"Oh Bob, I'm so glad you've called."

"Why? Is something the matter?" he asked. "You haven't been getting those funny phone calls, have you?"

"No; I thought it might be the police."

"The police? Has something happened?"

"You could say so. Oh, I'm so glad you're back, darling. Can you come over? I need to talk to you."

"Of course, but what's happened? Are you all right? You haven't been in an accident, have you?"

"No, no," laughed Judy, "I'm fine, but something did happen on the tube this morning."

"All right, Jude. I'll just have a quick shower and I'll be right over. Would you like me to pick up a Chinese, or have you eaten?"

"That would be lovely, Darling. See you soon."

Robert Knightly was a forty-year-old solicitor, specialising in company law, and his work involved a fair amount of travelling. He was divorced and had a ten-year-old daughter who lived with her mother in Derbyshire. He had met Judy at a dinner party some eighteen months earlier, and their relationship had quickly developed into a solid partnership. At thirty-eight years of age, Judy had endured several ill-fated love affairs, but had never felt as secure as she did with Robert.

Judy was in the kitchen when she heard Robert at the door. She ran to greet him, throwing her arms around him, and without saying anything he picked her up and carried her into the living room, smothering her with kisses.

"Stop silly! I can't breathe!"

"How can I stop now? I haven't seen you for almost a week!" he complained.

"I know, darling, it seemed like a month to me! I hate it when you go away." Then, tearing herself away from his embraces, she jumped up and went into the kitchen.

"I'll just warm it up in the microwave, darling; I hope you got some spring rolls, I love those. Then I'll tell you what happened this morning."

"But, Jude, don't you love me anymore?" he groaned, grabbing her from behind as she opened the boxes from the takeaway.

"Oh, darling, you know I do," she cried, as his hands reached over her breasts. "I'm sorry, but I've had rather a shock today, and I'm starving hungry."

"All right, gorgeous," he said, as she turned to be kissed gently on the forehead, "we've got all the time in the world, haven't we?"

"Oh, you are wonderful, Bob."

"I know! Come on, let's get some food inside us, then you must tell me what's happened."

Bob followed Judy into the kitchen, as they cleared away the remnants of their meal.

"Something happened on the tube this morning, you said?"

"Yes; actually it was two things."

"Well, come on, start with the first," he urged.

As they relaxed on the sofa, Judy turned to Bob.

"Firstly, Darling, would you believe me if I told you that I had a double?"

"A double? Do you mean someone who looks just like you?"

"Yes, exactly like me; in fact the spitting image of me."

"Good Lord! And was she on the tube with you this morning?"

"Yes, for a short while. She was standing with her back to me, so I didn't see her face at first, but she was the same height and build as me, her hair was blonde, and she was wearing a red coat similar to mine."

"How weird. And did she react when she saw you?"

"She didn't see me, thank God!"

"Why thank God? Didn't you want her to see you?"

"No, not after what happened. She had been standing quite near to me, but it wasn't until she jumped off at the next stop that I saw her face through the carriage window, and it shook me rigid. It was as though I was looking at my reflection in a mirror!"

"Yes, I suppose that would have been a shock; but where do the police come in? She didn't throw herself under the train or anything, did she?"

"No, it was worse than that. I think she killed

someone!"

"What?" cried Bob. "You surely don't mean she killed someone on the train?"

"Oh yes, the man standing next to me. Now do you see why I'm a bit uptight, darling?"

Bob stared at Judy. "This is incredible Jude! Are you telling me that a woman who looks like you killed somebody on the tube right next to you?"

"That's exactly what I am telling you, darling."

"Now, let me get this straight, Judy; what makes you think she killed someone? I mean, you didn't see her do it, did you?"

"No, but I'm pretty sure it was her."

"Just a minute, Jude, I can't quite take this in. You'll have to tell me everything that happened from the beginning, and I'm going to take some notes, if you don't mind."

"Good idea, because if the police arrest me, I'm going to need some help." Bob put his hand to his head and gulped down some more wine.

"Oh, come on now, Judy, it's not going to come to that, surely. Now just tell me calmly exactly what happened."

"All right; I'll start at the beginning."

When Judy had finished carefully narrating all that she had seen and heard that morning, Bob was looking very concerned.

"I can understand now why you are worried, Judy. I assume that the police are treating all the passengers as suspects?"

"Oh, yes they are, but if one of them describes the woman in the red coat, they will obviously see that the description fits me." Bob jumped to his feet.

"You weren't wearing yours today, were you?"

"No, thank God."

"I'm going to ring a friend of mine now, Judy," he said, "because if the police want to question you again, you may need a good lawyer."

"But Bob," she objected, "surely you can look after me?"

"You know I can't, Jude; I'm a company solicitor, and what you need is a good criminal defence lawyer."

"Oh Lord! Do you really think I'm going to need a lawyer, Bob?"

"I most certainly do, especially as you seem to have got it into your head to conceal evidence from the police. You must not answer any more questions until you have spoken to my friend. Do you understand?"

"Yes, Bob, all right. I'll do as you say."

Bob picked up the phone as Judy went into the kitchen to make some coffee.

"He's coming over," he announced.

"What now? It's nearly half past ten!"

"Never mind. I've explained the situation, and he agreed that he should see you straightaway."

"Oh Lord!" muttered Judy. "What's he like? Is he an old fuddy-duddy?"

"No, he's certainly not that," laughed Bob. "He's the same age as me, and he's a brilliant advocate."

"But what should I tell him?"

"You must tell him everything you told me, including your feelings about this woman."

"That'll be difficult," she sighed. "He'll probably think I'm a nut case."

"No he won't; he'll just think, as I do, that this double business is affecting your normal good sense."

Judy turned towards him, her eyes filling with tears. "But don't you see Bob, I really do believe that the girl in the red coat could be my twin sister. I don't know why, and I know it may not make any sense to you, but it just hit me when I saw her face."

"Oh come on, Judy, that's ridiculous! You know you were an only child," he said, exasperated, as he folded his arms around her. Judy shivered, turning away to wipe her eyes with a tissue.

"Thank God I've got you to look after me, darling," she said. "The policeman was here to question me again just before you phoned, so I could be arrested at any moment."

"What policeman?"

"The one who was there this morning. He was on the tube this evening, and he walked back with me."

"Was he alone?"

"Yes."

"Are you sure he was a policeman, Judy?"

"Of course," she laughed, "I'm not that stupid. He was taking statements on the station this morning."

"And has he taken one from you?"

"Yes, he's written everything down in his notebook, twice," she replied with a sigh. "But I didn't let on that I thought the man knew the woman, and certainly not that he had mistaken me for her!"

"Do you realise what you are getting yourself into, Judy?" cried Bob. "How can you be sure that no one heard him calling you by her name?"

"I can't," she replied. "But I'm not going to tell the police anything more until I have found out who she is, and if she really did stab the man." Bob stood up, to turn angrily towards Judy.

"I'm sorry, Judy, but I think you are behaving extremely unwisely. We both know you haven't killed anyone, and if you start hiding important evidence from the police, you will end up in deep trouble."

"I know, but I can't help it, Bob. That girl is a part of my past – I just know it, and I have to find her. I can't betray her to the police until I know more about her." Bob sighed, struggling for the right response.

"Oh Judy, Judy, I've never seen you like this before, and I'm at a loss to know what to say to you. It's as though you've experienced some sort of a revelation. But I'm not going to tell you to pull yourself together and be sensible; I'll leave that to Henry."

"Thank you for that," she replied. "I know it all sounds absurd, darling, but that's that way I feel. I just can't help it."

"Let's finish our coffee, and wait to see what Henry has to advise," said Bob wearily. "He should be here any minute now. I am sure you will like him; he's very kind and extremely practical."

"What's his name?"

"Henry Crofton," replied Bob, as the doorbell rang.

Judy's meeting with Henry Crofton went well enough, although he was obviously not happy with her decision to withhold some of the morning's incidents from the police. Despite his professional reticence, he listened patiently to her story, before warning her that, in the event that she were to be accused, he could not agree to defend her unless she agreed to reveal everything she had seen and heard that morning to the police.

Judy understood his attitude, and reluctantly accepted his counsel.

CHAPTER FIVE

Georgie couldn't get any sense out of the hysterical Suzanne. All that she had gleaned from her was that she had seen Graham, the boyfriend who had walked out on her, and that they must have had some sort of a fight. It was obvious that she would learn no more until Suzanne had calmed down.

Georgie and Suzanne had become friends in New York. Graham Cutler worked for the same bank as Georgie, and she had introduced him to Suzanne at a party. She had followed Suzanne's relationship with Graham from the beginning, over two years earlier, when Suzanne had fallen in love with him, but, to Georgie, Suzanne's idea of love seemed more like an obsession. Georgie had tried to warn her friend that she was heading for trouble, but Suzanne wouldn't listen. When Georgie's contract with the bank had terminated the previous year, she had decided to spend some time in Europe, and in particular in England to visit her English relatives. When Suzanne had found out that Graham had recently been transferred to London, she had gone berserk, and in a frantic email to Georgie, had confided that she had lent him seventy thousand dollars to help him to repay various debts.

Georgie was amazed. She had no idea that Suzanne had any capital, but, despite realising that she knew nothing about her friend's background, she was determined to stand by her. When Georgie had opened the door of her rented flat one morning a week earlier to find Suzanne there, she knew that she had come to find Graham, and that spelt trouble.

It was late afternoon when Suzanne awoke with a headache. The tranquilisers that Georgie had made her take had finally done their job, and she had slept for nearly six hours. Georgie was in the living room when Suzanne wandered in, dragging her feet, her eyes still swollen.

"Hello!" she muttered, as she plonked herself down on the sofa. "How long have I been sleeping?"

"All afternoon," replied Georgie. "Thank goodness I had those pills with me, otherwise I would not have known what to do with you."

"Was I that bad?"

Georgie felt a nervous tremor run down her back. "You were, and I'm not surprised," she said, turning to look straight at her friend. "I know what you've done, Su!"

"What do you mean?" stammered Suzanne.

"I found the knife. It was sticking out of your bag when it fell off the bed," announced Georgie coldly.

"Shite!" muttered Suzanne, as Georgie continued.

"Now that you've come to your senses, Su, you'd better tell me exactly what happened, because, whether you like it or not, I am involved in whatever you have done."

"Shite!" swore Suzanne again. "All right, I'll tell

you."

By the time Suzanne had finished recounting how she had followed Graham onto the tube that morning, and her efforts to get him to talk to her over the past few days, she was again almost hysterical.

"So you decided to kill him because he wouldn't talk to you? Have you gone completely mad?"

"I didn't decide to kill him," yelled Suzanne. "I didn't decide anything. I wanted to hurt him, that's all. I wanted to hurt him for what he's done to me!" she was again sobbing uncontrollably. Georgie stared at her friend.

"I don't believe you, if you didn't intend to kill him, what were you doing with my kitchen knife in your handbag, just tell me that?"

"I don't know, I just picked it up – I don't know why."

"I don't believe you," snapped Georgie. "I don't know what to say to you. I'm completely at a loss to understand. But something will have to be done. Surely you must know how badly you hurt him? Didn't he yell, or try to defend himself?"

"No, he didn't. I don't know what happened. I didn't see anything. I just jumped off the train. The last time I saw him he was reading his newspaper."

"But what if you killed him? That's what you said, isn't it? Why did you say that?" demanded Georgie.

"I don't know. I was just frightened."

Georgie stood up, shaking her head in despair. "Well whether he is dead or not, Su, you have committed a crime, and the police are bound to know about it, so what do you propose to do?"

"Perhaps I'll just get on the next plane back to New

York."

"That's ridiculous!" cried Georgie. "You'd be arrested before you got to the check-in. You'll have to give yourself up."

"Oh no, I couldn't. They'd hang me!" screeched Suzanne.

"For God's sake, Su, you'll have to do something, and quickly, because, friend or not, I have no intention of being deported for harbouring a criminal."

"Well, thanks a lot! I'd better go now," retorted Suzanne, marching back into the bedroom.

Georgie sank down onto an armchair her head in her hands. "Look, Su, come and sit down, and let's talk this out calmly," she said. "You can't just go rushing off like that. Somebody may have seen you on the tube with Graham, and the police may already have a description of you."

Suzanne jumped at her friend's words. "Oh my God! There was somebody! She was staring at me after I got off the train."

"Oh no! Are you sure?"

"She looked familiar. I think I know her from somewhere. Jesus! I think I've got a sister, Georgie!"

CHAPTER SIX

After returning home from work the following evening, Judy picked up her car and left for the local supermarket. It was Friday, and as she had arranged to spend Saturday with her friends and visit her mother on Sunday, she needed to do her week's shopping.

Sainsbury's was crowded as usual, but she shot round the aisles quickly, and was halfway down the last section, when a trolley suddenly slammed painfully into the back of her legs.

"Ow!" she exclaimed, "that hurt. Can't you look where you're going?"

"YOU, it's you!" screamed the woman wielding the trolley, as she pulled it back to launch it furiously again towards Judy, who this time, managed to jump out of the way. Judy stared in horror at the red-faced woman who continued screaming abuse.

"You killed him, you bitch!" she yelled at Judy, as nearby shoppers scattered in all directions.

"What the hell are you talking about?" shouted Judy.

Her attacker looked quite young, perhaps about the same age, and she was well-dressed, although totally hysterical.

"She's the one!" yelled the frenzied woman at the

horrified onlookers. "She killed my boyfriend. Call the police. It's her – look! Her picture's in the paper!"

Judy stared at her assailant in disbelief. "You're mad!" she shouted, at which the screaming woman rushed at her.

"I'll get you, you bitch, you'll see!"

"Of course I haven't killed your bloody boyfriend!" retorted a now red-faced Judy, as she backed away, her arms raised to protect her face.

A burly security guard appeared and, grabbing the girl from behind, pulled her away from Judy, her arms locked behind her.

"Let me go!" she yelled, kicking and struggling but the guard held her firm, her shouts fading to loud sobs as she was led away.

"My God!" muttered Judy staring after her.

"Are you all right, Madam?" asked a male voice beside her. Judy turned to recognise the supermarket manager. "Did she hurt you? I think your heel is bleeding."

"Oh, I don't know," stammered Judy. "I think I'm all right, thank you. It gave me such a fright. I've no idea who she is. She must be mad."

"Would you like to sit down?" he asked kindly, taking hold of Judy's arm.

"No really, I'm all right. I've finished my shopping, so I think I'll just get home."

"Well, if you're sure you can manage," he said, as he pushed her loaded trolley to the head of the queue, and began to unload her supplies. "I'll help you to your car."

"Oh no, please; you're very kind, but I'm sure I can manage now, thank you." And turning to escape the sea of staring faces, Judy limped out of the supermarket.

With her mind in a whirl, Judy had trouble remembering where she had left her car. She said my picture's in the paper! What on earth did that mean? Then she realised what must have happened. Someone must have told the police about her double, and they must have printed a picture of her in the paper.

"Damn!" she muttered, aware that she had forgotten to buy one that evening. Now what's going to happen?

Judy had wandered round the car park twice, the rusty wheels of her trolley going in all directions, before she finally located her car.

She opened the boot to unload her shopping, and was just heaving a ten-kilo sack of potatoes out of the trolley, when she heard a movement behind her, and before she could turn, something hit the back of her head, knocking her sideways. Without thinking, Judy automatically swung the heavy sack of potatoes around, felling her assailant to the ground.

"What the hell...?" yelled Judy shaking with anger, as she glared down at the girl cowering on the ground.

"Now I'm going to call the police! Who the hell are you, anyway?" The girl glared up at Judy, her swollen eyes shining defiantly.

"Go on, go on, call them, that's just what I want. You killed him and you're going to pay for it!"

Judy shook her head in despair. This was a nightmare. Why couldn't she just get in the car and go home? But she couldn't leave the girl like that. "Look, get up; I can't talk to you like that."

"I don't want to talk to you!" screamed the girl.

Judy felt like clobbering the girl again, but she was determined to control the situation. "Just get up!" she ordered, holding out her hand. "At least give me a chance to explain something to you."

"Explain? Explain what?" yelled the girl. "How you killed Graham!"

"For God's sake, shut up and listen. I haven't killed anybody, do you understand? It's all a terrible mix up."

While the girl continued sobbing and mumbling, Judy grabbed her firmly by one arm and pulled her to her feet.

"Please," she said, as she opened the car door, "calm down. Come and sit down and let me tell you what happened."

"I don't need you to tell me what's happened," sobbed the girl, as she stood up to face Judy.

"Just listen, will you?" Judy repeated, holding her firmly at arm's length. "I was on the tube, but it wasn't me that killed your boyfriend, you must believe me. Now please, let me help you, you are completely overwrought."

The girl started to sob uncontrollably as she collapsed over the bonnet of Judy's car. Judy reached out and gingerly placed an arm around her.

"Look, there's a café over the road, and we could both do with a cup of tea, then I'll explain about the photo."

"All right, but I'm still going to call the police because I know it's you in the paper."

"Oh, come on, let's go," sighed Judy, as she helped the exhausted girl across the road.

Luckily the café was almost empty, and Judy led the girl to a rear table and ordered two strong teas.

"What's your name?"

"Jean," said the girl, as she pulled out a tissue to wipe her nose. "I'm sorry," she mumbled, straightening up in her chair. "I just flipped, seeing your picture, and then, there you were right in front of me…"

"I understand, really I do. Losing your boyfriend like that…" She broke off as Jean burst into tears again. "Please, Jean, just let me try to explain. I haven't seen the paper this evening, but I can imagine what it is that is upsetting you."

"I've got it here," interrupted Jean, scrambling into her shoulder bag to pull out a crumpled *Evening Standard*.

"See? It's you! It must be," she cried, jabbing her fingers at the photograph at the top of the page.

Judy stared in horror at the picture, her heart beating wildly. It was almost an exact replica of her recent passport photo! And worse, in heavy print over the picture were the words: 'Have you seen this woman?' *Oh God!* she thought. *Half of London must have seen it by now. What on earth am I to do?*

Quickly scanning the wording underneath the picture, Judy read that a woman wearing a red coat had alighted from the tube at Victoria, and was wanted for questioning by the police in connection with a stabbing on the Victoria Line.

"That's it!" she exclaimed, pointing at the paper. "It obviously isn't me."

"Of course it's you!" cried Jean.

"Listen Jean; as I told you, I was on the train, but I wasn't wearing a red coat, and I didn't get off at Victoria. I was standing next to your boyfriend when he fell, and a doctor and a policeman were there too. I am sure they will both confirm that it isn't me they are looking for."

"But I don't understand. How come they've put your picture in the paper?"

"It's not me in the picture – that's just the problem. It's someone who looks like me!"

"What?"

"That's right," continued Judy. "There was another girl standing on the other side of your boyfriend, and she was wearing a red coat and got off at Victoria. I was there, of course, but when I saw her face through the window, I couldn't believe my eyes. She looked exactly like me!"

"What?" yelled Jean again, her eyes now flashing angrily. "Is this some sort of joke?"

"No it is not, I only wish it were. I know it sounds ridiculous, but it's true. It gave me the shock of my life when I saw her."

Jean stared open-mouthed at Judy, her face a picture of utter disbelief.

"I don't know what to say, you've totally floored me."

Judy couldn't help smiling as she replied. "Good, then we're quits. I've got a little of my own back then. Now, if you still want to call the police, Jean, that's fine by me, but they've already interviewed me twice."

Jean remained silent now, shaking her head, as she reached for another tissue. "I can't take this in," she murmured. "You don't really expect me to believe that, do you?"

"Perhaps not, but it's the truth, I assure you. Why don't you give me your phone number, Jean, and I'll call you on Monday."

"Whatever for?"

"Because I shall be worrying about you, and if you will agree to meet me again, we can have another chat."

"What's the point?" moaned Jean. "I don't want to

see anybody. Graham's dead, and I can't think about anything."

"Please Jean, I would like to help you."

"Oh yes, and how do you think you can to do that?" retorted Jean.

"Please Jean, here is my address," said Judy, handing Jean a slip of paper. "Why don't you just come round for supper on Monday evening?"

Jean stood up, shaking her head. "I don't know."

"Give me one good reason why not," insisted Judy. "Come on, Jean, you owe me an apology, and I owe you an explanation. Let's get to know each other, and I'll tell you what I plan to do."

"Plan to do about what?"

"About finding my double, that's what," replied Judy. "I hope you will come on Monday, Jean, I really would like to help you."

"I don't understand why you are being so nice to me. I'm perfectly all right now."

"I'm sorry, I only want to help." Judy was feeling embarrassed. "But I do hope you will come, Jean. About eight o'clock will be fine, and I shall look forward to that." As Jean turned to leave, Judy caught hold of her hand. "Take care of yourself, Jean," she said.

CHAPTER SEVEN

When Judy arrived home with her shopping, her heart sank as she noticed the light on her answerphone flashing. *Now all my friends will have seen that picture in the paper! How on earth am I going to explain all that to them and will they believe me?*

Then feeling quite exhausted, she sank down onto the sofa, vowing to ignore the phone. But it rang immediately, and continued almost nonstop for the next hour, by which time Judy had almost reached screaming pitch. Furious, she unplugged the lead from the wall socket, went into the bathroom and lit a row of scented candles. *At least here I can relax and try to clear my mind,* she thought.

Judy had slipped into a light sleep as she lay in the hot, steamy water, when she was startled by a loud hammering on the flat door.

"Judy, Judy, it's me!" she heard in the distance. She sat up wondering if she had been dreaming. Before realising that it was Bob calling her.

"Hell!" she exclaimed, as she hauled herself out of the water and stumbled to the door, clutching a towel around her.

"All right, Bob, just a minute. I was in the bath," she

shouted.

"Good God, Jude! Whatever's the matter?" he exclaimed, as she burst into tears.

"You know damn well what the matter is! I was just hoping for a bit of peace and quiet, that's all."

Bob stared at her askance. "Well, if that's how you feel, Judy, I'll go. Sorry to have disturbed you!"

"Oh no, Bob, don't go! I'm sorry, it's not you. It's just that I've had enough, with that picture in the paper and everything."

"I know, I've seen it, and that's why I'm here, Judy. Come on, let's get you dry and then I'll make you a cup of tea," he said, wrapping his arms around her.

"I don't want a cup of tea, Bob. I just want to get back in my lovely bath and forget everything."

"What, me too?" he teased.

"No silly, of course not." Judy giggled, a skittish smile lighting her face, as she dropped her towel to stand naked before him. "Come on, you old square," she chided, springing to life to pull his jacket from his shoulders.

"Steady on, Jude," he objected, hanging on to his trousers as she pushed him through the bathroom door. "I don't' want a bath, I want to talk to you."

"Well then, what better place to do it, darling?" she replied laughing.

Up to her neck in bubbles, Judy sat between Bob's legs as he massaged her back.

"What's this bruise, gorgeous?" Bob was gently fingering a purple mark on her shoulder.

"Oh, that's nothing. You should see the bump on my head and my swollen heel!"

"Now what's happened? You haven't been in an

accident, have you?"

"Not exactly. More of a fight really."

"What!"

By the time Judy had finished recounting her tussle with Jean at the supermarket, the bath water was almost cold.

"Do you realise, you could have killed her with those potatoes?" said Bob, as they dried themselves and returned to the living room.

"And what about me? She was so out of her head, she might have killed me!"

"Well, thank goodness she didn't; but you're not really going to meet her again, are you?"

"I hope so. It's funny, but apart from feeling sorry for her, I rather liked her."

"Now Judy, to get back to the picture in the paper," said Bob, taking charge half an hour later. "I've already spoken to Henry about it."

"Oh yes? And what did he suggest I do about it?"

"There's nothing you can do. The police are obviously aware of your concern, but you can hardly blame them for the fact that it may have been your double who killed the man."

"But what about my friends, and all the people in the office? They are all going to think that I'm wanted by the police! My phone never stopped ringing when I got home, that's why I unplugged it. How long will I have to go on explaining to people that I've got a double, and what if they don't believe me? It's a nightmare."

"It might not be a bad idea if you take a few days off work."

"Oh no! I couldn't do that. That would make it worse. Everyone would think that I'd been arrested or gone into hiding, or something."

"All right. Why don't you just record a message on your answerphone to stop people from jumping to conclusions?"

"Good idea."

On Saturday morning, Judy set off to meet her friends, Pat and Sandy. They had arranged to meet at a riverside pub at Kew, and when Judy arrived, she was greeted with some surprise.

"So you made it!" remarked Sandy. "I've been trying to call you, but your phone was off. We thought you'd been arrested."

"Oh please!" moaned Judy. "Don't you two start!"

Then, having told them all that had happened to her over the past few days, they promised to say no more about it. It was Pat's birthday, and after a rather liquid lunch, the three girls strolled round Kew Gardens in the winter sunshine, making plans for their holiday later in the year.

CHAPTER EIGHT

It was pouring with rain when Judy woke late on Sunday, but as she was determined to talk to her mother that day, she left immediately after lunch for the drive to the Surrey nursing home.

Mary Hay had been unwell ever since Judy could remember. She had suffered from severe bouts of depression when Judy was a child, and had endured several stays in psychiatric hospitals, but in her late fifties, she had been diagnosed with the onset of Alzheimer's. Judy had no memory of her mother being well and active, and consequently had never achieved a close and loving relationship with her. Her parent's marriage had soldiered on until her father's premature death some ten years earlier, when Judy had been obliged to sell the family home to finance her mother's enforced stay in a private nursing home.

Despite the lack of a close bond, Judy felt fond of her mother, and visited her regularly every two or three weeks, although each visit was now becoming more distressing as Mary's mental condition deteriorated.

As Judy drove up the long drive to the Georgian mansion which housed the nursing home, she wondered if this might be the day when Mary would fail to recognise her.

Mary Hay was sitting in an armchair looking out of the window when Judy knocked on the door and walked into her room. She was pleased to hear some music being played on the radio.

"Hello, Mummy," she said cheerily, as she walked round the chair to greet her mother. Mary's head turned jerkily towards her visitor.

"Is that you, Judy?" she asked, her blue eyes blinking in the light.

"Yes, it's me," replied Judy, as she pulled up a chair to sit down slightly in front of her mother. "How are you today?"

"Oh, I'm all right, are you all right, Judy?"

"Yes Mummy, I'm fine. I'm glad you're listening to some music; you've always liked Mozart, haven't you, Mummy?"

"Did I?" replied Mary vaguely. "We had roast chicken today, I like that."

"Mmm, so do I." *Oh dear, this is not going to be easy,* thought Judy, as she gazed out of the windows at the gardens. The trees were bare of foliage, but the colours of the chrysanthemums and the scarlet Pyrocantha hedge reminded her of the garden that her mother had once so carefully attended.

There was a knock on the door and a nurse came in. "Would you like a cup of tea, Miss Hay?"

"Yes, that would be lovely, thank you," replied Judy, wondering how she could bring up the subject of her birth.

"As Judy helped her mother with her teacup she said, "Mummy, there is something that I would like to ask you."

"Yes, dear?"

"Can you remember when I was born, Mummy?"

Mary's whole body began to shake as her teacup fell to the ground. "Uh, uh, uh," she stuttered through clenched teeth.

Judy felt the blood rushing to her face. *What have I done?* she thought, as she jumped up to put her arms around the trembling woman.

"Are you all right, Mummy?" Judy was unsure if she should call the nurse when Mary's right hand suddenly shot out towards her.

"What – what do you want? Who are you?" she stammered.

"Mummy, it's me, Judy, it's all right," she said, squeezing Mary's hand. Mary sighed, sinking back into her chair, now calm again. Dare I ask her again?

After the nurse had collected the teacups and mopped the floor, Judy braced herself for another try.

"Mummy, do you not want to talk about it?"

"Talk about it," Mary repeated, staring vacantly out of the window.

"About when I was a baby?"

Mary's head started to jerk again. "Baby, baby... baby," she cried, rocking from side to side.

Judy took a deep breath before continuing. "Was I born in hospital, Mummy?"

"Hos, hos, hospital," muttered Mary.

"Yes, Mummy, was I born in hospital?"

"What? What do you want? Who are you?" Mary was shouting now, her head shaking from side to side. "Go away... go away!"

Oh, it's no good, I can't get anything out of her, thought Judy despairingly, as Mary lapsed into silence.

"Mummy?" Judy tried once more. "Do you remember Daddy?"

"Daddy? Where is he?" demanded Mary, looking anxiously around the room, and back again towards Judy.

"No, Mummy, he's not here, but was he here when I arrived?"

"Arrived? Arrived here?"

"No, Mummy, not today. Was Daddy with you when I was born?"

Mary had turned to stare wide-eyed at Judy, her lips moving silently, as though repeating Judy's words. Suddenly her mouth fell open and she fell forward in her chair, her body again convulsed with jerking movements.

"Baby, baby…bb born?" she mumbled, as her head shot down towards the floor. Judy leaped up to grab Mary's arms. Then Mary started to scream.

"Hell!" exclaimed Judy wheeling round to reach the alarm bell on the wall.

"What's happened?" asked the nurse as she rushed into the room. "You haven't upset her, have you?" A second nurse came in and helped her to lift Mary onto her bed.

"I'm sorry, I'm really sorry," said Judy. "I don't know what happened. It must have been something I said."

"Yes, you have upset her, haven't you?" remarked the second nurse, as she prepared a small syringe to inject into Mary's arm.

"She'll need to have a good sleep now, and I suggest that you speak to the doctor before you leave, Miss Hay."

"Yes, of course," agreed Judy, as she bent down to kiss her mother goodbye. But Mary was already falling asleep.

"Do you think my mother is deteriorating, nurse?" asked Judy, as she followed the nurses from the room.

"The doctor will tell you, but she does seem to be going downhill more rapidly now," was the reply.

"I'm so sorry," said Judy again, as they parted in the corridor.

Judy drove away from the nursing home, certain that she had lost her only chance of finding out anything about her birth. The doctor had confirmed that something traumatic had obviously sparked off the illness which had robbed her mother of a normal life, and Judy of a warm and loving mother. Why had Mary kept murmuring 'baby, baby'? And why the complete block when she had asked about her birth? The more she thought about it, the more she became convinced that there must have been another baby, her twin sister.

Judy had arranged to meet Bob that evening, but when she arrived home, she felt depressed, and couldn't face going out to a restaurant.

"Can we spend the evening here, darling? I really don't feel like going out tonight," she told him on the phone.

"What again?" he remarked.

"And I need to talk to you about what happened today."

"Oh no! You haven't been clobbering people with potatoes again, have you?"

"No, of course not, silly. You know I went to see my mother."

"Oh, I see, it's that. I hope it wasn't too bad, Jude. I can be there about eight, is that all right?"

"Of course, and thank you, darling. I'll have dinner ready."

"What is it, gorgeous?" asked Bob, when he arrived to embrace her. "How was your mother? She's not…?"

"No, of course not; not yet anyway, but she's all over the place. She recognised me when I arrived, but later, she didn't seem to know who I was, and she kept telling me to go away. It wasn't very pleasant."

"No it couldn't have been much fun, Jude, but did you manage to have a conversation with her, or was she completely mazed?"

"I tried, but it was no good. When I asked her about my birth she closed up completely and started jerking, as though she was having some sort of fit, and she kept mumbling 'baby, baby' again and again. It was frightening. I thought she was going to fall, so I called the nurse."

"Oh Judy, you surely must have realised that would upset her?"

"No, I didn't, not really. Of course I know she has been ill ever since I was little, but I have to find out if it was because of something that happened when I was born."

"But Judy, you can't just go barging in upsetting her like that! It could drive her right over the edge!"

"But don't you see, Bob? Something happened that drove Mummy almost mad, and it must have been something really shocking. Post-natal depression is one thing, but for it to affect someone like that, and all but ruin her entire life; I mean, there surely had to be something else? The more I think about it, Bob, the more I am convinced that there must have been another baby, and that something happened to it."

"Oh come on, Judy!" exclaimed Bob, exasperated.

"You really are letting your imagination run riot. You must stop thinking about this twin business or you will make yourself ill!"

"But how can I, with a picture of my double all over the newspapers?"

"All right, Judy, admittedly you saw someone who looks like you, but it really is not so impossible. After all, you surely can't believe that among the millions of Caucasian women in the world, there is not at least one who resembles you?"

"Oh Bob, I thought that you at least would understand."

"I understand," he said sternly. "I understand, Judy, that you have had a bad fright, and as a result, you now believe that you may have a twin sister, but you can't just go rushing off upsetting your mother like that. You should at least have talked to the psychiatrist and let her deal with it. But, more importantly, Judy, you seem to have forgotten that this girl who looks like you has killed someone, and is still at large! Has it not occurred to you that she may think you saw her stab the man?"

"Do you mean that you think I could be in danger?"

"Well, of course! Surely you realise that, Judy? You were there when a man was stabbed on the tube and, from what you told me, it seems obvious that it was your double who did it. She must have seen you standing there, and perhaps even saw you looking at her after she got off."

"No, she didn't, I'm sure. She was turned away from the train, that's why I only saw three-quarters of her face."

"Well Judy, perhaps now you will forget this crazy idea that she could be your twin, and agree to do what Henry advised. You must tell the police everything!"

CHAPTER NINE

Detective Chief Inspector McGregor had called his team together for a briefing. It was now four days since the Victoria Line murder, and their investigation seemed to be going nowhere. With the squad's superintendent hard on his heels, he was under pressure to make an arrest before the end of the week

The Criminal Investigation Department was housed on two floors of one of the West End's oldest police stations, and despite being furnished with the latest computer technology, it was not a pleasant place to work. Maps, charts and pin-ups covered the peeling, cream-painted walls, while the fifty-year-old iron radiators hissed and spluttered like old steam trains.

The Georgian sash windows were permanently closed, nailed up to keep out the roar of traffic outside, while the air reeked of unwashed coffee cups and powerful aftershave lotion. The duty officers were rarely at their work stations, preferring to abandon their monotonous paperwork to follow up enquiries outside.

"Ah, so you've decided to grace us with your presence today, Jones?" remarked McGregor, as Detective Sergeant Jones walked in with his partner, Detective Constable Leary, carrying two mugs of coffee.

"Right then, what have we got; anything?" commented McGregor. A young woman constable stood up.

"We finished last night following up on the last of the commuters in the carriage, Sir, but so far, no one has come up with anything new."

McGregor walked over to a large plan pinned to the wall. "So, we have here ninety-two people at the scene of the crime, four of whom were standing near to the victim," he said, pointing to the green pins representing their positions in the carriage. "Are you saying that none of these four saw or heard anything unusual?"

"Not quite, sir," said Leary. "We have statements from two of them describing a woman wearing a red coat who was standing next to the victim. They noticed that she only travelled one stop, from Pimlico to Victoria, where she got off in a great hurry. It was only minutes later that the victim fell."

"And so far, we have had no response following our appeal in the *Standard*," interrupted Jones.

"The picture appeared in the paper on Friday, did it not?" remarked McGregor. "So it being a weekend didn't much help, did it? Still, I find it difficult to believe that no one has come forward to identify the woman, don't you? We'd better get the picture in again this week. Now, what about the passengers waiting to get on at Victoria? Who has been following up on them? Someone must have seen her get off! And we should surely be able to find someone who was walking behind her when she either left the station or changed to another line? I want you all to work on this in two groups, one in the tube station, and one around the main line area. Post pictures if you have to, emphasising the red coat. Someone must have seen in which direction she was heading. And don't forget the taxi rank: you'll need to check the drivers working that morning, all right? I want some results, and quick!"

McGregor sat down on the centre table, frustration written all over his tired face.

"Now, what about the victim, Graham Cutler? Have we found any connection yet between him and the woman? I presume you have shown her picture to his family and friends?"

"Of course," replied one of the officers, "but so far, no one claims to recognise her. We are waiting to hear from New York on that, because he was working over there until quite recently."

"How long was he over there?"

"That's just the problem, Sir. His bank said he'd been there for nearly four years."

"Great! That's all we need," snapped McGregor.

"To get back to the tube passengers, Sir," said Jones, "there is just one thing bothering me. It's the Hay woman, who was standing on the other side of the victim. There is something not quite right there."

"Ah, yes, Miss Hay," said McGregor, frowning. "I had a call from Henry Crofton, the lawyer, about our picture. Apparently it's almost identical to Miss Hay's passport photo, and she's afraid she will be mistaken for the suspect."

"That's interesting, Sir," remarked Jones, "because I'm convinced that she knows something, and anyway, why does she need a lawyer if she has nothing to hide?"

"Have you taken a statement from her?"

"Of course. I interviewed her first on Thursday morning, and again at her flat that evening, and she was adamant that she hadn't noticed the suspect, or anyone else."

"She was there, was she not, standing right next to Cutler?"

"Oh yes, she was the one who called for help when he fell, and she was on her knees holding his hand when the doctor and I arrived."

"So, if she is worried about our picture, she must look very similar," observed McGregor.

"That's just the problem, Sir; it looks exactly like her!"

"And you think she knows something, do you, Jones?"

"I'm certain of it, sir. Apart from anything else, she denied even seeing the woman, even though she was standing just two or three feet away from her."

"Mmm, you may be right, Jones. I think we'd better follow up on Miss Hay. See what you can find out about her family, will you? Has she got a sister, or a twin perhaps?"

Jones' face lit up. "That could be it, Sir! If she looks so similar to the red coat woman, then she could be her twin, in which case, she'd be trying to defend her!"

"That is possible I suppose, but it's a bit far-fetched, don't you think?" said McGregor, a wry smile crossing his face. "Just don't waste too much time on it, Jones, although you should perhaps pay another call on Miss Hay."

"Will do, thank you, Sir," said Jones, as the meeting broke up.

Judy arrived home earlier than usual that evening. She was pretty sure that Jean would not turn up, but decided to make a bolognaise sauce which she could always use up during the week. Having given up on Jean by half past eight, she had just put some spaghetti in a pan to cook when she was startled by the doorbell.

"Hello!" said Jean, as Judy opened the door. "I'm sorry I'm late. I wasn't sure if I should come."

"Why ever not?" asked Judy, smiling, as she took Jean's coat.

"I wasn't sure if you really meant it, I thought you were just being nice," said Jean, blushing.

"Nice? Why would I be nice after you almost crippled me in the supermarket," teased Judy.

"Well, you were kind to me, after you'd floored me with your potatoes!"

Judy laughed.

"Come on in, silly. I've made some spaghetti bolognaise. I hope you like it."

"Yes, I love it."

After their meal, the two girls carried their coffee into the living room.

"Let's sit down and I'll try to explain about the picture in the paper," said Judy. "I really did mean it when I said that I could understand how you must have felt when you saw me in Sainsbury's. It must have been quite a shock! A bit like the shock I had on Thursday morning."

"No, it couldn't have been much fun seeing Graham dying right next to you," remarked Jean, her eyes now brimming with tears.

"Oh, I'm sorry, I didn't mean that. I didn't mean to upset you," said Judy, taking Jean's hand in hers.

"What did you mean?"

"I was thinking of the shock I had when I saw my

double through the train window. It gave me such a fright!"

"Oh, your double," sighed Jean. "The woman you say is in the picture?"

"That's right."

"But nobody has a double, Judy. I mean, surely the only way someone else could look exactly like you would be if she was either an identical twin or a clone!"

"Exactly!"

"Don't tell me that someone has grown a clone of you from a piece of fingernail or something?" mocked Jean.

Judy laughed. "Of course not."

"So are you telling me that she is your twin sister?"

"That's what I believe, and I'm going to find out."

"What do you mean, 'believe'? How could you not know if you had a twin sister?"

"That's the trouble, Jean, I don't know."

"Before you confuse me anymore Judy, won't you tell me what happened on the tube, please. I must know how Graham died," pleaded Jean. "Did he cry out when he was stabbed?"

"Oh no, Jean, it wasn't like that at all," replied Judy, placing a comforting arm around the distressed girl's shoulders. "One minute there he was, standing reading his newspaper, and moments later, he was on the floor. I thought he had just fainted, I'm sure he didn't suffer it must have been very quick."

"But didn't you see what happened?"

"No. It was such a shock when the policeman said he was dead. The woman in the red coat had got off at Victoria, and we were halfway to Green Park when he fell."

"Was there a policeman on the train?"

"Yes, with the young doctor who tried to save him."

"How? What did they do?"

"When I called for help, this young Indian doctor appeared, and started to give him heart massage," said Judy. "That was when I thought he'd had a heart attack."

"So by the time they realised that Graham was dead, the woman had long gone?"

"That's right."

"But didn't he know what was happening to him? Didn't he regain consciousness at all?"

"He did seem to come round for a moment when he fell," replied Judy. "I knelt down to try to comfort him."

"Oh, if only I'd been there!" sobbed Jean.

"Oh Jean, I'm so sorry," said Judy. "Perhaps I shouldn't be telling you this."

"Oh please, I must know. What happened then?"

Judy took a deep breath before continuing. "When I looked at him, he opened his eyes for a second, and he mistook me for her!"

"Who?"

"The woman in the red coat."

"Do you mean your double?"

"Exactly. He looked straight at me and called me 'Suzi'." Suddenly Jean was on her feet, staring open-mouthed at Judy.

"SUZI? Did you say Suzi?" she yelled.

"Yes, Suzi, I'm sure. Why?" asked Judy, startled by Jean's obvious agitation.

"Tell me exactly what he said," urged Jean. "Did he say anything else?"

"No. Oh Jean, it's so difficult to explain; I don't want to upset you anymore."

"Go on PLEASE, Judy!" Jean was almost shouting. "I must know. Are you sure he said Suzi, or was it Suzanne?"

"No, it was Suzi, I'm sure. I was holding his hand when he opened his eyes, then he sort of whispered from the back of his throat…"

"Yes, yes, go on!" urged Jean.

"Suzi no, he gasped, then the doctor arrived and…"

"JESUS!" yelled Jean. "It was HER! She must be in London!"

"What are you talking about? Don't tell me you know who she is?"

"Oh yes, I know who Suzi is," replied Jean, "and now I know who killed Graham!"

Judy stared in disbelief at Jean, who was by now pacing furiously up and down the living room.

"But how can you be sure it was her?" Judy's heart missed a beat. "Nobody saw her do it; it might have been somebody else!"

"If Graham said 'Suzi', then it's obvious. It was Suzanne. She's killed him!" yelled Jean.

Judy felt suddenly sick. My God! So now it seems there is no doubt that she killed the man! She took a deep breath, steeling herself to continue. "Calm down, Jean," she pleaded. "Come and sit down and tell me who this Suzanne is."

By the time Jean had finished telling Judy about the problems Graham had had with Suzanne Greenberg, the neurotic girl he had been engaged to in New York, Judy could no longer kid herself that it could have been someone else who had killed him. The girl she believed to be her twin sister was a killer! Judy shivered, remembering how she had felt at the sight of her on the tube.

"Are you all right?" asked Jean, peering anxiously at Judy's blood-drained face. "You look terrible!"

"Thanks, yes I do feel terrible," she replied, smiling bravely. "Do you realise what you have just told me, Jean?"

"Yes. That I know who killed Graham."

"But she's my twin!" muttered Judy, holding her head in her hands.

"Oh Judy, for heaven's sake, you mustn't think that! Maybe she does look like you, but she's a psychopath!"

"It was when I saw her face, I just knew who she was," whispered Judy.

"But that's crazy! How can you possibly believe that when you only saw her for a second through a window?"

"It wasn't just that. I can't explain it, and I know it may not make any sense, Jean, but she seemed so familiar, and I had such a strange sensation that I knew her from long ago."

"But Judy, were you adopted?"

"No, I wasn't, and even if I had been, I know that my parents would have told me."

"Are you sure? Perhaps they thought it better that you didn't know."

"No I wasn't, I'm certain."

"Then what about brothers and sisters, have you got any, and are they like you?" Jean was struggling to find an explanation.

"No, I was an only child, and I do look very like my mother."

Jean stood up, shaking her head despondently. "This is getting beyond me."

"I'm sorry," said Judy, "you probably think I'm

mad."

"No I don't, but I wish I could understand what has made you so certain that Suzanne is your twin. Graham never mentioned that she had been adopted. And anyway, even if she was your twin, how would that help me? You'd be bound to want to protect her."

"Would I? I wonder. She's a complete stranger to me."

"Then why do you want to find her?"

"I don't honestly know. I suppose I just need to know if she really is my twin, and why we were separated."

"But what if you did find out that she was your twin; would you really want a murderer for a sister?"

"Of course not. Let's not talk about it anymore, Jean. I think we could both do with a drink."

"You're right there!" agreed Jean. "Although I'll have to go soon."

Judy fetched the half bottle of wine left over from their meal.

"You've got me so confused, Judy. I just don't know what to think," said Jean, as she sipped her wine. "But you must forget all about Suzanne, or you will cause yourself untold heartbreak. All I want is for the police to find her, whether or not she is your twin, and I shall do all I can to help them."

"Of course you do, I understand that, and at least when they find her, everyone will stop thinking it's me they are looking for! I am sure the police suspect me of something, anyway," moaned Judy.

"Perhaps they think she is you twin too, and that you are trying to protect her," remarked Jean. "Have they been here yet?"

"Only once, on Thursday."

"So they know you are not hiding her then?"

"Good grief! I hadn't thought of that!" exclaimed Judy. "That's all I need; a bunch of them crashing in here with a search warrant! I'd better warn Henry."

"Who's Henry?"

"He's my lawyer. My boyfriend said I would need one."

"Because of the picture in the paper?"

"That's right. You're not the only one who thought it was me!"

It was almost eleven o'clock when Jean left, and Judy picked up the phone to call Bob. But there was no answer, so she decided to call Henry Crofton. His phone rang eight times before he picked it up.

"I'm sorry to be calling so late, Henry," she said. "I do hope I'm not disturbing you."

"Not at all, Judy, I was reading up on a case before going to bed. Has something happened?"

"Yes," she said. "I know who killed the man on the tube!"

"Good Lord!" exclaimed Henry. "How on earth?"

"I've just spent the evening with his girlfriend, Jean, and when I repeated the name he'd whispered, she couldn't believe it. It was the name of a girl he had been engaged to in New York!"

"Good God!"

"And what's more," Judy continued, "he had dumped her because she had become impossibly neurotic and suicidal, and he had told Jean, that she often wore red clothes."

"My goodness me, what an extraordinary coincidence! But hadn't the girlfriend recognised her from the picture in the paper, Judy?"

"How could she? Suzanne was in New York, and Jean had never seen any photos of her, but as soon as I mentioned her name, Jean realised who it was. From what Graham told her, Jean is convinced that Suzanne is mad, and probably came to London to kill him!"

"Then you must tell the police, Judy!" urged Henry. "I should give them a call right now, if I were you."

"I suppose you're right," she replied, thinking she'd do it in the morning.

"Let me know how you get on, Judy."

"I will," she replied.

CHAPTER TEN

Georgie woke up and looked at the bedside clock. It was twenty past six in Friday morning, and she had slept for less than three hours. She rolled slowly out of bed, her head throbbing.

"What the hell am I to do?" she muttered to herself, as she slid her feet into her mules. She had tossed around in bed nearly all night, going over and over the scene with Suzanne the previous evening, and she felt exhausted. How on earth was she to extricate herself from the predicament she found herself in? She padded silently into the bathroom, struggling to think calmly. If Suzanne refused to go to the police, then she would have to leave. She would help her to get away from London, then it would be up to her. She could do no more. Friend or not, she was not going to get herself chucked out of England for sheltering a murderer!

There was no sound from the guest room, and Georgie guessed that Suzanne would sleep for several more hours after the strong dose of sleeping pills she had made her take. After a quick shower, she hurriedly dressed and left the flat, quietly locking the door behind her. She grabbed a passing taxi and went straight to Selfridges.

It was almost midday when Georgie returned to the rented flat, her American Express card spent almost to its limit. She had purchased an entire new wardrobe for Suzanne and, as she laid out the clothes in the living room, she felt certain that anyone who had seen Suzanne on the tube would never recognise her in the far from stylish navy coat, and the natural-looking brunette wig she had managed to find.

Whether Suzanne would be pleased or not, she didn't care, but she hoped that she would at least try to understand her reasons for not wanting her to stay.

Georgie picked up the rail ticket to Glasgow that she had bought, and knocked on the guest bedroom door. There was no answer. She knocked again but there was still no response. Suddenly afraid that she may have overdone the sleeping pills, she opened the door and went in. Georgie stood staring at the rumpled bedclothes, unable to move. Suzanne was not there!

"Hell!" she muttered. "Where is she?" She slammed the door shut, a feeling of panic rising in her stomach, as she rushed across to the bathroom.

There were two wet towels on the floor, and as she walked over to the hand basin she noticed some splotches on the mirror and traces of a dark strain around the basin.

"Oh no!" cried Georgie. "She's used my hair colour and scarpered, where the hell has she gone? Oh Suzanne, you bloody fool!"

Georgie had hired a car on her arrival in England, and her first reaction was to dash out and drive around, in the hope of spotting Suzanne, but she soon figured out that it would be a waste of time. Suzanne would hardly be likely to remain out in the open for longer than absolutely necessary. Fighting off the remorse over her anger the previous day, Georgie reminded herself that, whatever may happen to Suzanne now, she could in no way be held responsible. Suzanne alone would have to face the consequences of her vicious attack. But what if she really had killed Graham? Georgie shuddered. Surely not. She couldn't really have killed him, could she?

Georgie was in despair. She didn't know what to do, or what to think. Perhaps the beautiful, slightly crazy girl she had known in New York really was crazy: perhaps she was mad! After all, she really knew almost nothing about Suzanne's past.

She had never spoken about her family or, come to think of it, about her life before she came to New York. Who was she really?

The telephone rang, bringing Georgie sharply back to reality. She grabbed the receiver, thinking that it must be Suzanne, but it was her cousin, calling to confirm arrangements for the weekend. Georgie had so looked forward to spending several days with her cousins on the Cotswolds, but she regretfully had to postpone her visit. She felt obliged to stay in London in case Suzanne returned.

CHAPTER ELEVEN

The following Tuesday morning, Judy was sitting in John's office taking notes for some letters he wanted her to write, when the phone rang on her desk outside.

"Leave it, Ducky," he said, "they can put it through here if it's urgent." Moments later, it rang on John's desk.

"Yes?" he answered sharply. "No, she can't, she's busy. What? The police?" he exclaimed, glancing over towards Judy. "All right, you'd better send them up."

"Oh no! They've come to arrest me!" cried Judy.

"Don't be silly, Judy." John stood up and walked over to the door. "I'll deal with them. You just sit tight."

Several minutes later, John returned, followed by Detective Sergeant Jones and Detective Constable Leary.

"It's all right, Judy; the officer just wants to ask you a few more questions about last Thursday."

"I'm afraid I will have to ask you to accompany us to the station, Miss Hay," announced Jones.

Judy felt her pulse racing as she stared up at John.

"Is that really essential, Officer? You are welcome to use my office," said John.

"That won't be necessary, sir," replied Leary. "Come along Miss Hay," he added, as he held the door open.

Judy glanced back fearfully towards John.

"Don't worry, Ducky, you'll be back here in no time," he said with an encouraging wink.

Judy followed the two policemen out of the building, painfully aware of the staring faces around her. They'll all have seen the picture in the paper, and now they'll think that I'm the murderer!

On their arrival at the police station, Jones offered Judy a seat by his cluttered desk. She sat down, gazing around the dismal room while struggling to remember what she had told him before. Jones was impatiently jabbing his index finger onto his computer keyboard.

"Now, Miss Hay, what have you got to tell us? Have you managed to drag anything else up from the depths of your memory?"

Judy sat up sharply, bristling at the policeman's sarcasm.

"You have already interviewed me twice, Detective Sergeant, and I have nothing further to tell you," she retorted, struggling to remain calm and in control.

"That was not the impression I had after our last chat, Miss Hay. I believe you are holding something back from us, and as this is a murder enquiry, you would be well advised to tell us what it is."

"I'm sorry, but I don't know what you expect, I've already told you everything I know," she replied, thinking, *Oh Lord, now I am getting into deep water*.

Judy sat up, summoning her most confident voice. "Look Officer, I don't understand why you have brought me here, you must surely realise that I didn't kill that man! I would hardly be likely to be hanging around if I had, would I? And now, thanks to that picture in the paper, all my friends think it is me you are looking for."

"It was stated quite clearly that we want to question a woman in a red coat who alighted from the train at Victoria, and we all know that wasn't you.

"Now, Miss Hay," continued Jones, "what about this woman who looks like you? As far as we're concerned, she could be a relation, perhaps even your sister."

Judy's heart missed a beat. "Oh really, Sergeant! That's ridiculous because I haven't got a sister; I was an only child."

"Are you quite sure, Miss Hay? People don't have doubles you know."

"Well, I seem to have one!" snapped Judy. "And believe me, when I saw her face it gave me the most terrible shock."

"Ah, so now you're saying that you DID see her, are you?"

"Who?" muttered Judy, weakly.

"The woman in the red coat," snapped Jones.

"Yes, I did see her after she got off the train," admitted Judy. "But I don't see why you are looking for her in particular. There were lots of other people there, and she wasn't the only one who got off at Victoria. Are you going to publish all their pictures in the paper, too?"

"Now, come along, Miss Hay, you have already denied seeing the woman; what else have you conveniently forgotten to tell me?"

"I do have something that may perhaps interest you, Sergeant," said Judy, the blood rushing to her face. "Thanks to your picture, I was attacked in the supermarket on Friday evening."

"What?"

"Yes, by someone who thought it was me in the paper, and I might have been badly injured."

"What do you mean by 'attacked'? Did somebody hit you?" The policeman was sounding almost sympathetic.

"If it's of any interest to you, Sergeant Jones, I was assaulted by a supermarket trolley, and then clobbered over the head in the car park!"

"What? Hit on the head? Who did that?" he demanded.

"It was a totally hysterical girl, Sergeant, who was convinced it was me in the picture. I don't suppose it has occurred to you to interview the victim's girlfriend?"

"His girlfriend?" Jones swung round in his chair. "That's the first we've heard mention of a girlfriend! Are you sure it was his girlfriend?"

"Oh yes, quite sure," replied Judy. "And now I'd like to get back to my office, if you don't mind, Sergeant."

"I'm sorry, Miss Hay, but I'm afraid that's not possible. I will have to detain you for further questioning."

"What?" cried Judy. "But you can't keep me here, I haven't done anything."

"Oh, yes I can, Miss Hay," he replied. "What you have done is to withhold certain information appertaining to a murder enquiry, which translates as obstructing the police in the course of their investigation. You have already been less than truthful by denying that you saw the woman in the red coat, and now you announce that you know the victim's girlfriend! In the circumstances, I have every right to keep you here until you agree to be more cooperative."

Judy stared across the desk at Jones, her anger rising. *The bastard!* she thought.

"Well how long do you intend to keep me here?" she demanded angrily. "Because I am not going to answer any more questions until I have spoken to my lawyer."

"Ah, your lawyer!" mocked Jones. "The famous Mr Crofton, although I don't quite understand why you should think you need a lawyer, Miss Hay, if you are, as you say, an innocent bystander." Judy grimaced, raising her eyes upwards. "All right, Miss, you may call your lawyer. You can use the phone over there," he added, pointing to an empty work station.

"Do you have a phone directory? I don't have his number on me," said Judy warily.

"Perhaps you'd like me to dial it for you?" muttered Jones, his patience now wearing thin, as he tapped into his computer.

It was over an hour later when Henry Crofton arrived at the police station to be shown into the interview room where Judy was waiting.

"They haven't charged you, have they?" asked Henry, concerned.

"No, thank goodness, but they said I'm obstructing them in their investigation, and that they have a right to keep me here!"

"That's quite correct, Judy, but why are you obstructing them? You have told them what you told me last night, haven't you?"

"Not yet," she admitted.

"Why ever not, Judy? I advised you to call them straight away. Why did you not do it?"

"I thought it would be best to leave it until this morning, then, before I had time to call them, they arrived at my office," she replied, feeling rather stupid.

Henry was looking far from happy. "Have you forgotten what I told you, Judy? You know that I cannot act for you unless you agree to disclose everything you have told me to the police. I believe I did make that quite clear."

"You did," she agreed, "and I thought you understood my reluctance to incriminate the woman who I believe to be my twin."

"But, Judy, you know now that it is highly likely that she killed the man! The police are already looking for her, so it's only a matter of time before she will be apprehended, so you must tell them what his girlfriend told you."

"I know you are right, Henry, but it's so difficult."

Henry leant forward across the table towards Judy. "Look, Judy, from what you told me last night, I would say that it is highly likely that this Suzanne did kill the man. How can you be sure that she won't do it again?"

"I can't," sobbed Judy.

"Do you want me to represent you, or not, Judy?"

"Yes I do."

"Good. So you do now agree to tell the police everything that you saw and heard on the tube that morning, Judy, and what the girlfriend told you?"

"I don't really have much choice, do I?" sighed Judy.

"Not unless you want to be charged with obstruction, Judy. This woman, Suzanne, is obviously unstable and probably dangerous, whether or not she is your sister, and I strongly advise you to put this twin business right out of your mind, at least until the tube killing is resolved. After that, if you decide to continue with your research, just remember that you could spend the rest of your life visiting her in prison! Is that really the sort of relationship you would wish to have with a twin sister?"

"No, of course not!" cried Judy. "But how can anyone be sure it was her? Nobody saw her stab him, and the police haven't found the weapon, so what proof do they have? All they know is that she was there, and that she left the train in a hurry like everyone else. What if it wasn't her?"

"I give up," sighed Henry.

"I don't," said Judy.

"Judy Hay, you are the most obstinate woman I have ever met!" said Henry, a wry smile crossing his face. "I'll have a word with the Chief Inspector now, then it'll be up to you, but for heaven's sake Judy, don't go giving them the impression that you are trying to defend her, otherwise we may not be able to get you out of here." Henry knocked on the door, and followed Leary out of the room.

Judy remained seated, her head in her hands. She felt stupid and very tired. Henry must think I'm a complete idiot! Perhaps I am, but I still believe that that woman, or Suzanne if it is her, is my twin, and whatever anyone else thinks, I am going to find out if my mother did give birth to twins. If Suzanne is my twin, she may be unhinged because of something that happened when she was born, or perhaps, there is a gene on mummy's side of the family which caused her mental ill health and Suzanne's too!

Detective Constable Leary walked back into the interview room. "I've brought you a cup of tea, Miss," he said, as she placed a plastic beaker on the table.

"Thank you. Do you think I'll be here for much longer, Constable?"

"That's hard to say, Miss. Detective Sergeant Jones will be in to take a new statement from you shortly."

It was almost one o'clock by the time Judy and

Henry left the police station.

"Well, I'm glad we've got that sorted out at last," he remarked, as he took Judy's arm. "You had me quite worried there for a while, Judy, but thank God you took my advice! You must be feeling a lot better now that you've got it all off your chest. Robert will be pleased."

"I suppose so," said Judy, "but that inspector made me feel like a right worm, ticking me off like a naughty child."

"Well, I hate to say it, Judy, but you had it coming, and I did warn you."

"I know," she murmured, "and you were right, of course. I'm sorry I was such a pest, Henry, and I really am grateful for your help."

CHAPTER TWELVE

When Judy arrived at the tube station the next morning, she found that the trains were not running, due to a slight snowfall during the night. It was quarter to ten when she finally arrived at work, having stood shivering at the bus stop for over half an hour. Christmas was only a couple of weeks away, and the office was already half empty with some of the staff away on holiday, and others at home with flu. John was nowhere to be seen so, as it was their quietest season, Judy decided to do a thorough clear out of his office. First stop though was the coffee machine, then, pulling open all the filing drawers, she grabbed the bulging files and slung them into several piles on the floor. Realising what she had let herself in for, she picked up the phone to make a couple of personal calls before setting to work.

Pat answered the phone in the small jewellery boutique where she worked. "Judy! Thank God you've called. I've been worrying about you. Have they caught the murderer yet?"

"No, they're still looking for my double, but at least I'm off the hook now, or I hope so."

"Why? Have they been to interview you again?" asked Pat.

"No, but I had to go to the police station yesterday."

"Jesus! They didn't charge you, did they, Judy?"

"No, of course not. Henry persuaded me to tell them everything, including my scuffle with the girlfriend."

"Who on earth is Henry?"

"He's a lawyer friend of Bob's, and he agreed to defend me if I was accused."

"Good, so now perhaps you can relax and stop worrying about your double."

"Perhaps, but whatever she may have done, I still can't help believing that she is my twin."

"Oh come on, Judy, you must forget it."

"I'm not sure that I can now, not after the way my mother reacted when I saw her on Sunday."

"Why? Did she tell you something?"

"Not exactly, but she… oh Pat, John's just arrived, I'll have to hang up."

"Come on, Judy, you can't leave me in suspense like that, you must tell me the rest! Meet me in the sandwich bar at one thirty."

"Fine, I'll be there," said Judy.

"Hello, Ducky!" greeted John, as he threw off his heavy sheepskin coat. "Lovely day, eh? The bloody car wouldn't start. Have I missed anything?"

"Not a thing," replied Judy. "There's hardly anyone around, so I thought I'd have a go at sorting things out."

"So I see," he groaned, as he stepped over the files on the floor. "Now I'll never find anything!"

"That's just the point," laughed Judy. "By the time I've finished sorting this lot, you will no longer have the excuse for being late for your meetings because you couldn't find the papers!"

"Don't nag, woman!" he remonstrated, as he went

out to fetch a coffee.

Pat was sitting on a high stool at the counter when Judy arrived at the sandwich bar.

"Sorry I'm late. I'm having a spring clean at the office. What are you eating?"

"Oh, just a toasted ham and cheese."

"I think I'll have a salt beef and a large cappuccino," said Judy, turning to the girl behind the counter.

"Come on now, what's all this about your mother? What did she tell you?"

"She didn't tell me anything, but she reacted so disturbingly when I asked her about my birth, that it was obvious that something traumatic must have happened. It was awful. I had to call the nurse and they sedated her, so I had to leave."

"Poor you. It must be terribly upsetting to see her like that," said Pat.

"It is, and I know now that I will never be able to find out anything from her; she is going downhill fast."

"I'm sorry," said Pat.

"It's strange," Judy continued, "but I have never really thought of her as my mother, more of an aunt really. She was never there when I needed her, it was always her needing everyone else."

Pat squeezed her friend's hand. "It's when you hear stories like yours, that I realise how lucky I am with my family. My mother is more like a sister, in fact, she acts like a teenager sometimes!"

"You are lucky," said Judy, laughing. "But I think I may try to see my aunt in France, she's bound to know something. She was in England when I was born."

"Good idea, but I still think you could be making a

big mistake, Judy. What if your double does turn out to be your twin, and she did kill the man? How would you feel then?"

"I'm pretty sure now that she did kill him." Judy swung round on her stool to face Pat. "Remember I told you that I had asked the girlfriend to supper?"

"Yes, did she turn up?"

"Oh yes, and we got on really well. I feel terribly sorry for her; she was obviously in love with him, and is heartbroken."

"She would be, poor girl," said Pat.

"But wait till you hear what she told me!"

"Yes? Go on."

"She insisted that I tell her everything that happened, and when I mentioned the name her boyfriend had whispered, she recognised it immediately!"

"Do you mean when he mistook you for your double?"

"Exactly. It was the name of a girl he had been engaged to in New York last year."

"Good grief! So now you know her name! But is she sure, Judy? I mean, if the girl was in New York, what was she doing on the tube in London?"

"Jean was certain it was her, and I'll tell you why."

"Bloody Hell!" cried Pat, when Judy had finished recounting what she had learned from Jean. "And he called you Suzi! Well, there you are then, Judy. How can you possibly believe she is your twin? She must be insane! You must forget all about her."

"That's what everyone keeps telling me, but if I've got a twin, I want to know," moaned Judy. "I don't care what she's like, or even what she's done. I just can't help it."

"But what about Jean? What does she think? Surely she doesn't want you to find her?"

"Of course not. She'd probably like to kill her herself!"

"God, look at the time!" cried Pat. "I've got to get back to the shop, and I haven't told you about the tickets for the carol concert. You will come, won't you?"

"Of course, but couldn't we invite Jean? It might cheer her up a bit. I don't suppose she's been anywhere since it happened, and I'm sure you will like her."

"What a good idea. I'll call you to arrange where to meet," said Pat.

After work that evening, Judy caught a taxi to a West End wine bar that Bob had heard about. The taxi driver couldn't find it, and after driving up St Martin's Lane twice, Judy paid him off, deciding to find it for herself.

It was a freezing cold evening, and having walked the length of the road through slithery snow slush, she arrived breathless only to slip at the top of the steps leading down to the basement wine cellar. A tall, seductive-looking man caught her arm as she almost fell.

"Are you all right?" he asked, looking intently into her eyes. "You are all wet. You haven't been walking, have you?"

Judy blushed, shivering under his gaze. "Yes. The taxi driver had never heard of this place, so I didn't have much choice," she replied, as he led her down the stairs.

"What you need it a good stiff toddy," he said. "My name's James, by the way."

"Hello! I'm Judy," she replied, still blushing, as they walked into the crowded room.

"What would you like, Judy? A glass of mulled wine

perhaps?"

"That's very kind of you, James," she replied. "But I'm here to meet my boyfriend."

"Now that really is a pity," he said. "Never mind, perhaps another time?"

"Perhaps," she murmured, turning away, embarrassed, to look around the room.

"Judy!" cried Bob, as he caught sight of her. "I was getting worried. I thought you'd gone off with Henry."

"Why ever did you think that?" she exclaimed, as he kissed her gently on the cheek.

"He rang last night, and he's really taken to you, Jude."

"Really? I had the impression he thinks I'm an absolute fool. Mind you, if you hadn't been here it might have been James who I went off with."

"Now who the hell is James?"

"A very charming and sexy gentleman who helped me down the stairs. Now, how about some wine, darling? I'm frozen."

"Yes, you are a bit wet, Judy. Let's sit by the fire," said Bob, as he led her over towards a huge log fire roaring away in the centre of the cave-like room. "How about a good full Italian?" he suggested.

"Great!" agreed Judy, as she slipped out of her wet overcoat.

"How was your day, darling?" she asked, hoping to avoid any interrogation over her problems with the police.

"Pretty ghastly. I had a long meeting with a blue-chip client who thinks he knows more about the law than I do. But never mind me, Jude. Tell me about how you got on at the police station."

"Oh please, Bob! Couldn't we just enjoy one evening without bringing all that up again? Honestly, I'm sick and tired of thinking about it."

"But Judy, I just want to know how you got on. You know I've been worried about you."

"I'm sorry, darling. I really do appreciate your concern, but I'm all right, really. Surely Henry filled you in when you spoke?"

"He told me that you hadn't been charged."

"There you are then. There's nothing else to tell you. Can we change the subject? What's this wonderful film we're going to see? It's not another American police thing, is it?"

"No, it's most certainly not that. It's a comedy."

"Thank goodness. I could do with a laugh."

Bob stood up to pull an envelope from his briefcase. "Here's something to cheer you up, gorgeous."

"What is it?"

"Open it, then you'll see."

"I hope you're not giving me my Christmas present early; because if it is, I shan't open it," she ventured, as she fingered the envelope.

"All right then, I'll go on my own," he teased.

"Go where? What is it?"

"Just open the bloody envelope, Jude," said Bob, laughing as she tore it open.

Judy's mouth fell open as she pulled out two flight tickets.

"Oh Bob, how wonderful! I've always wanted to go to Madeira," she cried. "Are we going for Christmas?"

"That was the idea," he said, as Judy jumped up from her chair. "Thank you so much, darling. You really are amazing!" she cried, throwing her arms around him, as loud cheers and applause broke out from the tables around them.

"Now see what you've done," he moaned, looking around, embarrassed at the rowdy crowd.

"It's what you've done, darling," she replied, laughing.

"We're going for ten days, Judy, and I've booked us a suite at Reids," he announced, as the cheering died down.

"But Bob, that'll cost a fortune!" she objected. "You must be mad!"

"Well thanks. I'm glad you appreciate it," he mocked.

"Of course I appreciate it, darling. I'm sorry, it's just such a wonderful surprise."

"You deserve it, Judy, after all you've been through," he said. "And I intend to make sure that you relax totally, and forget all about that woman on the tube."

"I'll try, Bob, I promise."

"You'll do more than try if I have anything to do with it," he insisted.

"I can't believe it; I'm so excited!" cried Judy. "Just think, we may be swimming in the pool on Christmas morning, instead of looking out of the window at the pouring rain."

"Drink up then gorgeous, or we'll be late for the film!" said Bob, as he poured the last of their bottle of Barola into her glass.

CHAPTER THIRTEEN

The following Saturday, Judy with Jean took a taxi to the concert hall where Pat was waiting in the foyer.

"I'm so pleased you could come, Jean," greeted Pat warmly.

"It was good of you to think of me," murmured Jean.

"We're up on the second balcony," said Pat, as she led the way up the stairs. "Wow, there's no mistaking it's Christmas!" she exclaimed, staring up at the huge central Christmas tree. "And I haven't done anything about it."

"Neither have I," agreed Judy, adding, "oh I'm so sorry Jean; I didn't mean to upset you. It must be a terribly sad time for you."

"That's all right, Judy. I've never really enjoyed Christmas. In fact, I usually pretend it's not happening, and I wasn't with Graham last year, if that's what you were thinking. We'd only been together since July." Pat took hold of Jean's hand.

"Don't worry, Jean, we'll make sure you have a real Christmas this year, won't we, Judy?"

"I hope so," replied Judy, "but I'm afraid I shan't be here."

"What? You're not going away, are you, Judy?" exclaimed Pat, surprised.

"Yes, it's Bob's Christmas present. He's booked for us to go to Madeira, so we'll be leaving on Christmas Eve."

"You lucky bitch!" cried Pat. "Now why can't I find a man like that?"

"Oh, Judy, how lovely! How I envy you going off to the sunshine," said Jean.

"Never mind, I'm always on my own at Christmas, so you must come to my place, Jean," said Pat. "I'll cook a turkey with all the trimmings."

The concert was being performed by the Royal Choral Society and the Bach Choir, with the London Symphony Orchestra, and, as well as the traditional carols, the programme also included Bach's Christmas Oratorio and some modern orchestral pieces. The three girls were seated quite high up, and Judy was disappointed that she was unable to spot a friend who was singing in the Bach Choir.

The interval arrived all too soon, and while Judy sped off in search of some coffee, Pat and Jean joined the queue for the toilets.

"I really am enjoying myself, and I hope that Judy is feeling more relaxed now," said Jean.

"Oh Judy's all right, it's you we're concerned about," said Pat. "I really do feel for you, Jean. It must be unbearable to lose the person you love, and in such terrible circumstances. If you ever feel the need to talk about it, you know you can call on me at any time."

"Thank you, Pat. I may take you up on that one day, but at the moment I am just trying not to think about it. The worst part is not knowing where he is, and not being able to see him. I don't think Graham had told his family about me; they were so upset when they heard about

Suzanne, so I can't even find out when the funeral will be."

Pat reached out to fold her arms around the distressed girl's shoulders. "Come on now, Jean, remember what you said? Let's just concentrate on the music."

"I'm sorry. I'm all right really. If anything can help me, it's listening to music," said Jean, as she rummaged in her handbag for a tissue to wipe her eyes.

"I've got quite a collection of classical music at home, Jean. So we can have a musical Christmas, if you like."

"That would be lovely," replied Jean, as they returned to their seats.

Judy remained standing at the rear of the circle for a while to stretch her legs, before joining the others.

"There seems to be a lot of tourists here," she remarked, as she sat down. "Mostly American, I would say."

"What makes you think they are Americans?" asked Jean. "Do they look like that lot in *Dynasty*?"

"No, but I've heard them talking, and look at those women down there," said Judy, pointing to a group several rows below them, "they are all wearing heavy make-up and huge earrings."

"They probably have to cover their faces with thick Pancake to cover their facelift scars," remarked Pat.

"Oh, I thought everyone had 'Botox' nowadays instead of facelifts," added Jean, as the music started to fill the hall.

Judy continued to look around, and it occurred to Pat that she might still be looking for her double.

"Have you spotted your friend in the choir yet?" she

asked.

"No, we're too far away," replied Judy. "And anyway, she's an alto so she'll be several rows back."

The orchestra played the introduction to the final item on the programme, and the conductor turned towards the audience, inviting them to join in with the medley of traditional carols.

"Hark the Herald Angels Sing..." sang Judy and Pat at the top of their voices, while Jean silently mouthed the words feeling slightly embarrassed.

They were halfway through the last verse, when Judy suddenly stopped singing. Pat turned towards her, surprised, as Judy leapt to her feet, staring wildly down towards the front of the circle.

"Look!" she cried, pointing down over the head of the man in front of her. "It's her! She's here!"

"Who?" asked Pat, following Judy's stricken gaze. "Is it your friend?"

"Quick!" yelled Judy, as she struggled to push past the couple in the next seat. "She's down there. Come on!" Pat grabbed her arm.

"Judy for God's sake, shut up and sit down," she ordered, in a stage whisper, but she couldn't hold her. Judy was halfway along the row.

"What's the matter?" asked the man next to them.

"I'm terribly sorry," whispered Pat, as she followed Judy.

"What the hell are you doing?" muttered Pat, as they reached the steps. "You've disturbed all those people. Come and sit down," she added, making a grab for Judy's arm. But Judy wasn't listening.

"She's there, I tell you, down on the second row; can't you see her?" She was almost shouting as she

90

started down the steps. A uniformed attendant ran down from the back of the circle.

"What's the problem, Madam?" he asked Pat. "Is your friend ill?"

"It's all right, I'll manage. I'm terribly sorry," replied Pat.

"Just keep her quiet, will you?" he demanded. "Otherwise I shall have to ask you to leave."

"Of course," demurred Pat, as she set off after Judy, who by now, had almost reached the second row.

"For God's sake, Judy, come back!" whispered Pat, as she caught up with her. Judy turned towards Pat, her eyes blazing.

"Can't you see? It's her! Look, in the red coat!" she cried, pointing to a blonde woman sitting halfway along the row.

Oh my God, I must be psychic. *She thinks it's her double!* thought Pat. "For heaven's sake Judy, this is ridiculous! You can't go thinking every woman in a red coat is your double!"

"It's her, I know it is, and I'm going to have a look," announced Judy.

"Oh no you don't!" said Pat, grabbing her by the arm. "You just stay here and wait," she ordered. "I'll go down and have a quick look, and don't you dare move, or we'll have to leave."

Pat walked quietly down to the front of the circle, then slowly worked her way far enough along to get a good look at the woman. Moments later she glanced back at Judy, shaking her head. Judy started nervously down the steps to meet her.

"Well? It is her, isn't it?" she demanded.

"No Judy, it most certainly is not your bloody

double," announced Pat. "Now come and sit down!"

"But how do you know? Doesn't she look like me? Are you sure?" Judy was not giving up.

"She's an elderly, coloured lady with bleached blonde hair. So now I hope you are satisfied!" said Pat, now obviously annoyed. Judy stared disbelieving at her friend.

"Oh God, I'm sorry. I was so sure it was her," she mumbled.

The attendant met them on the stairs. "Would you please kindly return to your seats, ladies, as quietly as possible," he said.

"Of course," replied Pat, holding Judy firmly by the arm. "I'm so sorry about the disturbance."

"What was all that about?" asked Jean, as Pat and Judy regained their seats.

"Oh nothing at all," replied Pat, as the applause broke out, suppressing the need for further explanation.

CHAPTER FOURTEEN

Judy had almost dreaded returning to the miserable cold of London, but on the morning that she returned to work after her holiday, the West End seemed half deserted and she enjoyed the short walk from the tube station to her office. There were very few tourists about, and even the buses were running singly, instead of the usual clumps of three or more. John was still away, so before settling down to work, she went into the kitchen to make some coffee.

As she waited for the kettle to boil, she looked down at the sparkling diamond and sapphire ring on her finger, and her mind wandered back to Madeira, remembering the night in the hotel gardens when, before she had realised quite what was happening, Bob had slipped the ring onto her finger. *What would he have done if I'd said 'no'?* she wondered. But she knew that she could never have refused him. Later that night, under the shower, Bob had teased her that he would leave her if she started to worry again about an imaginary twin sister, and she had promised him that she would put the woman in the red coat right out of her mind.

Back at her desk, Judy noticed that two faxes had come in inviting tenders for a large amount of Gum

Arabic and a shipment of crop sprayers for Nigeria.

"Well, that's a great start to the New Year!" she muttered. "Where on earth am I to find all that Gum Arabic?"

Pat was waiting in the sandwich bar at lunchtime.

"Wow!" she exclaimed at the sight of Judy's suntanned face. "You look great!"

"I feel great, or I did till I got to work this morning," laughed Judy.

"Tell me all," urged Pat. "How was Bob? Are you two still talking?"

"Of course," replied Judy, waving her left hand in front of Pat. "Look!"

"Bloody Hell, Judy, you're not engaged?" yelled Pat, as she grabbed her friend's hand, her eyes fixed on the ring.

"I suppose I am."

"What do you mean 'suppose'? You must be if he's bought you a rock like that, Judy. You're not going to change your mind, are you?"

"Of course not," replied Judy, laughing.

"So when's the big day?"

"Oh, we haven't got to that yet; I don't even know where we will be living. Bob wants to get out of London, but I'm not sure. But tell me about your Christmas, Pat. Did you see Jean?"

"Oh yes, she spent Christmas Day with me, and I've seen her a couple of times since."

"I'm glad," said Judy. "I couldn't help thinking about her while I was away."

"She's spoken to the police," continued Pat, "and she thinks they will arrest that woman soon."

"Really?"

"They think she's still somewhere in London. They've found a red coat in the London Transport lost property store."

"But that could belong to anyone," remarked Judy.

"Perhaps, but they said it was bought in New York."

Judy shrugged.

"You're not still worrying about her, are you, Judy? Because if you are…"

"No, I'm not. I can't. I promised Bob," replied Judy, turning away.

The phone was ringing when Judy walked late into her office the following morning.

"Morning Ducky, where've you been?"

"Hello John," she replied. "Yes, I am late, I'm sorry, but it's dead as a dodo around here. There's nothing happening and I think I'm the only person in the building."

"Never mind, Jude, is there any post?"

"No, only a couple of faxes for tenders, and I can't do much about them; I've tried the usual sources but they're all closed till next week."

"Lock up and go home, Ducky. There's no point in hanging around," said her boss. "We'll start again next week."

"Oh great! Thanks John. I'll be early on Monday." As Judy replaced the receiver she realised that gave her almost another free week, and as Bob had driven north to see his daughter, she knew what she wanted to do.

Judy left the office and caught a taxi up to the London Records Office in Northampton Road. *If I have got a twin sister, then surely her birth registration will be next to mine,* she thought, as she feverishly scanned down the Hays on the screen. It didn't take her more than five minutes to find her own entry in the June quarter of 1952, but there was no other female Hay birth shown near her own.

Judy's heart sank when she saw the number of pages of Hays there were, until common sense told her that her twin's birth would only be shown in the same quarter as hers, or possibly the one after. But it was not there. Judy struggled on for almost an hour, vainly searching for an entry, before giving up in despair. I just *know* I've got a twin sister, she told herself, as she left the crowded building. There must be something somewhere. Then she thought of the hospital where she was born.

The following day, Judy drove to Winchester. She knew she had been born in Winchester General Hospital, but she had no idea if it was still there. It could have been closed down, or amalgamated with another. As she drove towards the town centre, she spotted a sign for 'Hospital', and following the directions, soon found herself in front of the huge Royal Hampshire County Hospital.

Judy parked her car and found her way to the main reception area. The woman on reception didn't know where she should go. She thought there must be an Archives Department somewhere, but had no idea where it was. She suggested that Judy should ask at the Maternity Clinic.

Some forty minutes later, Judy was told that patients' records were kept for only twenty years, and that the Archives were stored elsewhere. Perhaps she should try the Hampshire County Archives. Thoroughly disheartened, Judy returned to London. The County Archives would have to wait for another day.

That evening, after a long phone conversation with

Bob, Judy decided to call Jean, hoping that she may have heard something about Suzanne from the police.

"Oh Judy, how good of you to call," greeted Jean. "How was your holiday? Did you have a wonderful time?"

"Fabulous," replied Judy. "And I've come back engaged."

"Engaged? Do you mean engaged to be married?"

"Yes."

"Congratulations!" said Jean. "So now I bet you've forgotten all about having a twin, haven't you?"

"Not really. I tried to, but I can't."

"Listen, Judy," urged Jean, "the police came to see me again yesterday, and it sounds really bad, so you must forget all about Suzanne."

"Why, what did they say?"

"They made me repeat everything that Graham told me about her. They wanted to know if she had ever lived in Chicago."

"Why?"

"Because they've found something on internet unsolved crime records about a missing suspect fitting her description."

"But why Chicago?"

"Because the suspect was the wife of a wealthy man who was murdered there six years ago."

"Bloody Hell!" exclaimed Judy. "And had Graham ever said anything about Suzanne being married before?"

"No, he only told me how difficult she was, and the scenes they had. I really don't think he knew very much about her past. He never told me much, although he did say that she hadn't lived in New York for very long."

"Oh God!" murmured Judy. "So does that mean that

she may have killed two people?"

"Well of course," said Jean.

CHAPTER FIFTEEN

Judy walked out into Oxford Street. She had wandered around Marks & Spencer for ages, but hadn't bought anything. It would be her mother's birthday soon and she wanted to buy her a new bed jacket; perhaps she would find something in Selfridges.

"Su!" Judy jumped, startled, as somebody grabbed her arm. "Suzanne, where the hell have you been? Oh my God. "I'm so sorry. I thought you were someone else," muttered a woman in an unmistakable American accent.

Judy stared after her. Suzanne, she said Suzanne!

"Just a minute!" she shouted, turning to run after her. "Please wait. Did you say 'Suzanne'?" she asked, as she caught up with the smartly-dressed brunette on the crowded pavement.

Georgie turned towards Judy.

"That's right. I'm so sorry if I alarmed you, but you look just like me friend!"

"But you called me Suzanne!"

"Yes, that's her name," replied a puzzled Georgie.

"I'm sorry," said Judy, "but I must ask you something."

Georgie backed nervously away.

"Is your friend's name Suzanne Greenberg, by any

chance?"

"Well, how on earth do you know that?"

"Look," said Judy. "I must talk to you, it really is important."

"Yes, it must be if you know her. Do you know where she is?"

"No, I don't, but could we just go somewhere for a coffee? I really must talk to you."

Judy led Georgie round the corner to a small sandwich bar and ordered two cappuccinos.

"My name is Georgina Calcutt," said Georgie, introducing herself.

"I know that I look just like Suzanne," said Judy, "and you're not the first person to have mistaken me for her, but my name is Judy Hay, and I believe that I may be her twin sister."

"What! Su's got a twin?" exclaimed Georgie, staring across the table at Judy. "Come to think of it, you are *exactly* like her. So when did you last see her, Judy?"

"I only saw her once; I don't know her at all."

"Oh?" Georgie was baffled. "Was it recently that you saw her?"

"It was on the tube, when it happened," replied Judy. "I saw her face when she got off, and that's when I knew."

"Knew what?" asked Georgie.

"That she is my twin."

"I don't quite understand, Judy. Are you telling me that you saw Suzanne on the Underground?"

"That's right."

"What do you mean 'when it happened'?"

"When the man collapsed. I was standing right next to him."

"Jesus! So you saw her do it!" cried Georgie.

"No, I didn't see anything. Nobody did," said Judy. "He fell on my foot, that's all. The police are looking for Suzanne because she was standing next to him, and she jumped off at the next stop."

Georgie was staring at Judy.

"Are you sure? You really didn't see what happened? Didn't she speak to him or cry out?"

"No, but why are you looking for her?" asked Judy.

An hour and three coffees later, the two women parted with each other's phone numbers, Georgie having recounted all that she knew about Suzanne, and Judy having told her about her search and her meeting with Jean. Georgie was due to leave for Italy the following week, and was worrying about contacting the police, but Judy advised her against it, promising to tell no one of their meeting, or of Georgie's involvement.

That evening, after a long phone call from Bob, Judy decided to call her Aunt Constance in France. She felt sure that she would remember if something terrible had happened when she was born. After all, she was Mary's twin sister, and Judy knew that they had been close, at least until Constance had left her husband to run off to France.

Constance answered the phone immediately.

"Judy, my dear! I thought you'd forgotten me. How are you, and how is Mary?"

Judy made her excuses, then, after hearing about her aunt's frantic sounding social life, said, "Auntie, something strange happened to me recently, and I'd really like to talk to you about it. Is there any chance that I could come over one weekend, soon?"

"*Mon Dieu*! That does sound mysterious, Judy.

You're not in some sort of trouble, are you?"

No, not me Auntie, unless you consider getting engaged to be trouble."

"Oh, my dear, that is good news. I hope you've picked a good one."

"Oh yes, Auntie, he's wonderful!"

"Well Judy, of course you will be welcome, and I shall look forward to seeing you again. But can't you tell me what it is that you wish to discuss, does it concern Mary?"

"No Auntie, not Mary. She's in good hands, I promise. Would a weekend next month be convenient?"

"Of course, my dear. I believe there are a number of cheap flights to Toulouse now."

"Good, I'll call you when I can get away, Auntie, and thank you."

Judy lay awake that night, wondering if she would ever be able to find out if Suzanne really was her twin.

Even if her aunt did remember her birth and what had happened, would she be willing to talk about it, or would she clam up just as Mary had?

The next morning, Judy decided that she had to find out where the Hampshire archives were kept. It would be silly to dash back to Winchester if they were somewhere else. She found the phone number of Winchester's main library from Directory Enquiries and, ten minutes later, learned that the Records Office was in Winchester, and did in fact hold some hospital archives.

Several hours later, Judy was on the M3, headed back to Winchester. She drove into the town, and was about to stop to ask for directions when she realised that she was already on the right road. She pulled in to a nearby car park and stepped out into the rain. Wondering which end of the road the Records Office was, she opened up her umbrella and turned into Sussex Street. As she passed the theatre, she noticed a shabbily-dressed, elderly man standing looking at the photographs outside, while his fat-bellied basset hound plopped a large, wet turd onto the pavement.

"Excuse me," said Judy, grimacing. The man turned, startled. *I bet he thinks I'm a dog warden*, she thought. "Can you tell me where the Hampshire Records Office is?"

The man coughed. "You must have passed it; it's up there, by the car park," he said, waving his hand back up the road.

"Thank you," said Judy, backing away from his unpleasant breath; and avoiding the panting dog, she set off back to the car park.

It was almost an hour later when Judy finally reached the entries for 1952 in the Royal Hampshire County Hospital's archives. Taking a deep breath, she scanned down to the June records. There, beside her mother's name, she read that she had given birth to a female child at one thirty a.m., and to another female at two fifteen! Judy gulped, hardly able to believe her eyes.

"So I did have a twin, I knew it!" she muttered, her heart beating wildly as she read and re-read the words. The record stated that the first baby had weighed six and a half pounds, but there was no further mention of the twin. Why hadn't they recorded her weight? Judy's mind was racing as she sat frantically searching for something more, but there was nothing else about either Mary's condition or the second baby. *This is crazy*, she thought, *something must have been left out.* Her head in a whirl, Judy copied the entry into her notebook then, after quickly running through the June and July records once more, she returned to the enquiry desk, hoping that they may be able to furnish some sort of an explanation.

There was a long queue of people waiting to question the grey, bespectacled woman on the enquiry desk, and as Judy took her place, the tall man in front of her turned to look at her.

"Are you trying to trace your family?" he asked in a high-pitched, nasal voice.

"No, I'm not. I just came to check the birth records." Judy thought he was definitely rather odd. He had a completely bald head, a gold ring in one ear, and a scruffy beard.

"Oh, pity," he said. "I'm researching two Hampshire families for my thesis, and I'd be delighted to help you."

"Thank you, but it's not necessary," said Judy, as the woman beckoned him forward.

"How may I help you?" asked the young man who joined his hard-pressed colleague.

"I don't know if you can, it's rather strange," said Judy. "I came to check my and my twin sister's birth record in the hospital archives."

"Yes?" he asked.

"Well, it shows the weight of the first baby, but not that of the second."

"Is that important?"

"Yes it is," said Judy. "Because although it gives the times of each birth, there is no further mention of my twin."

"I'm sorry, but we can't be held responsible for the hospital's omissions," he said, sounding impatient. "We can only keep what is deposited with us."

"Yes, I know that," muttered Judy, "but I was just

hoping you could suggest what might have happened. I mean, is it possible that some of the records could have been lost?"

"It is entirely possible that the hospital could mislay or destroy old files," he said. "But that is hardly the case here, as you have found the entry of your birth. I suggest that you try the hospital," he added, turning to beckon the next person.

"Yes, well thank you," said Judy, not sure whether she should be feeling angry or embarrassed, as she turned away.

Judy felt both elated and let down. She knew now that her mother had given birth to twins, but what happened then? And why all the secrecy? Was something being hidden from her, or was it just a simple clerical error, in which case perhaps there never was a twin. Oh stop it, Judy! She told herself. I'm getting obsessed.

She was just leaving the building when the bald-headed man suddenly re-appeared beside her. *Oh go away!* she thought.

"Excuse me," he said, peering down at her, "but I couldn't help hearing what you said back there."

"Oh?" mumbled Judy.

"Forgive my asking," he continued, "but is your sister alive?"

"What?" exclaimed Judy, openly annoyed. "Of course she is."

"Ah – then that's no good."

"What do you mean? What are you talking about?" asked Judy.

"It had occurred to me, that the reason she is missing from the records could be because she was stillborn."

"Stillborn?" repeated Judy, incredulously.

"But as she's alive that doesn't apply, does it?"

"Certainly not, but thank you for trying," said Judy. And avoiding his outstretched hand, made a dash for the doors.

Judy set off back to London, feeling relieved that she had now at least achieved something, but before she had arrived back home, doubts had begun to cloud her mind.

Stillborn! She mused. That man said stillborn. If my twin was stillborn, that would, of course, have been a terrible shock for Mummy, and it would also explain my impression that I was a twin.

But if she was born dead, how would that explain my feelings on seeing Suzanne? I have never before in my life ever imagined that I could have a twin, so why did the sight of her affect me like that? And if Suzanne is not my twin, who is she, and why does she look just like me?

That evening Judy phoned Bob. She longed to discuss her worries with him, but knew that he would be angry if he knew what she was trying to do.

"What have you been up to, gorgeous?" he asked.

"Not much. John gave me the rest of the week off, as there was nothing happening at work."

"Oh Judy, why didn't you tell me? You could have come up here!"

"I don't think that would have been a very good idea; and anyway, I've been catching up on a few things here."

"Oh? And who's been keeping you away from me?"

"Don't be silly," laughed Judy. "You know I can't wait to see you again."

"Good, because I'm coming back tomorrow," he announced.

"That's great! I'll cook you a fabulous meal."

"I'll need it, Jude, after all that I've had to swallow

up here."

"Oh dear, was it that bad?"

"Pretty ghastly," he replied, "but Jilly is fine, thank God, although she seems more like her mother each time I see her."

Judy couldn't get to sleep that night. She was so looking forward to Bob's return, and although she longed to tell him about her two visits to Winchester, she felt she should keep her search to herself, for the time being anyway. She tossed from her side, onto her back, and back again a dozen times before finally, glancing at the bedside clock to see that it was half past two, she got up and went into the kitchen to make a cup of cocoa.

What is the matter with me? she wondered, as she sat with her head in her hands at the kitchen table. I've got everything I could want; my own flat in London, a steady job, and a wonderful boyfriend who wants to marry me, so why do I sometimes feel so alone, and why this shadow hanging over me? She thought again about the creepy, bald-headed man's suggestion. I've simply got to check whether it could be true, whether I like it or not, she decided. If my twin was stillborn, would that mean that she had never really existed? But if she'd died shortly after her birth, then there would surely be a death certificate.

CHAPTER SIXTEEN

The following two weeks passed quickly for Judy. She was suddenly very busy at work, dashing backwards and forwards to the Chamber of Commerce offices to get export licences stamped and approved for several big shipments she had arranged; and with her evenings totally committed to Bob and their future plans, she had barely given a thought to the missing twin.

Bob had arranged to meet Henry Crofton for lunch in the City one Friday, and asked Judy to join them. John was out of the office that day, and as Judy had finished all the paperwork for the week, she decided that after checking the post, she would take a couple of hours off. That would give her a chance to check the death records at the London Records Office before meeting Bob.

When Judy arrived breathless at the city restaurant, she looked far from happy. Bob noticed immediately that something was worrying her.

"You look rather distant, darling, is something the matter?"

"I'm not sure," she replied vaguely. "I'm rather confused."

"Yes, I can see that. What is it? Is it something I've done?"

"Of course not, darling. I'm sorry if I seem a bit pre-occupied, but please don't let it spoil our lunch, and I was looking forward to seeing Henry again."

"And I was hoping to find you rather more relaxed by now, after your lovely holiday, Judy," said Henry. "I hope you have succeeded in putting all that twin business right out of your mind."

"Oh dear," sighed Judy. "If only I could."

"Judy!" exclaimed Bob. "You promised!"

"I know I did, darling, but something's happened."

"What do you mean?"

"I'm sorry, Bob, I did try, but I'll have to tell you now, and you'll probably be delighted."

"The only way I'd be delighted, Jude, would be if you told me that the police have arrested that woman who looks like you, and proved that she is not your twin!"

"Oh, it's better than that."

"Well, come on Judy, don't keep us in suspense," urged Henry.

"She's dead," announced Judy.

"Dead? Well, that's great," said Bob. "Now you really can forget all about her, can't you?"

"So, how did you find out, Judy?" asked Henry.

"I've just seen the death registration of my twin sister at the Records Office," she said.

"But that's wonderful, Jude," cried Bob. "It proves that the woman you saw couldn't possibly have been your twin."

"I know," said Judy.

"So you really did have a twin after all," remarked Henry. "That's interesting."

"Yes," she said.

"And at least now you can stop worrying that you

may be the twin of a mad woman, Judy."

"Yes," she said again, as the waiter arrived with their hors d'oeuvres.

When the phone rang in Judy's flat that evening, Bob answered it. "It's for you, Judy," he said. "It sounds like an American."

"An American? I don't know any Americans," she said, as she took the receiver.

"Am I speaking to Judy Hay?" asked Georgie.

"You are," replied Judy. "Is that Georgina Calcutt?" she asked, suddenly recognising her voice.

"The very one," said Georgie. "How are you, Judy?"

"I'm fine. But what's happened, Georgie? Do you have some news?"

"Yes. I just got back from Italy yesterday, and I had a call from Suzanne this morning."

"Oh Lord," sighed Judy. "Where is she? Has she been arrested?"

"No, but she's hiding out in some man's flat in North London, and she wants to see me."

"Bloody Hell!" muttered Judy. "What are you going to do?"

"I'm going to meet her," said Georgie, "and I wondered if you would like to come with me?"

"Oh Lord! I don't know," said Judy.

"What's going on? Who is it?" asked Bob.

"It's all right, Bob," she whispered. "I'll tell you about it in a minute."

"Will you go?" she asked Georgie.

"Yes, I feel I should at least try to help her. Maybe she's ready to give herself up."

"Can I call you back?" Judy asked.

"Of course, take your time," said Georgie.

"I'll call you tomorrow," Judy promised, before hanging up.

"I assume you were talking about that woman you thought was your twin, Judy," said Bob, as they sat down.

"Yes, I'm afraid so," said Judy. "That was Georgie, a friend of hers. Suzanne was staying with her until she disappeared after the stabbing."

"How did you meet her?" he asked.

"I met her in Oxford Street, when she thought I was Suzanne, just like Jean in the supermarket."

"Oh dear, there seems to be no escape from that damned woman," moaned Bob.

"I'm sorry, darling," said Judy.

"But you have put it all behind you now, haven't you. Judy? I agree that it was strange that seeing that woman led you to believe that you had a twin, but now that you know that your twin is dead, there really is nothing more you can do."

"You're right, of course," said Judy. "But Georgie wants me to go with her."

"Go where?"

"To see Suzanne. She's still in London."

"You can't be serious, Judy?" he exclaimed. "Why on earth should you want to meet her? It's nothing to do with you now, she is *not* your twin, and she's probably a killer! If your friend Georgie wants to see her, that's up to her, but you mustn't have anything further to do with her, Judy!"

"I suppose you're right," said Judy.

"I know I am," he said. "And I will not have my gorgeous fiancée getting mixed up with a dangerous psychopath."

The following morning, Judy called Georgie.

"Are you really going to meet Suzanne?" she asked.

"I am," replied Georgie.

"But what if the police have traced her? You could be arrested."

"I know, but I'll be careful. Nobody knows she was staying with me, I'm sure, and I can't just abandon her."

"Georgie, I'm sorry, but there's really no point in my meeting her now," said Judy. "I've found out that she can't be my twin after all."

"Oh? Well, I guess that must be a relief in the circumstances, Judy."

"I suppose you're right. But when are you going to see her?"

"Tomorrow afternoon," replied Georgie.

That evening while Bob was out, Judy called Georgie. "I've changed my mind. I'm coming with you," she announced.

At two o'clock the next day, Judy called for Georgie at her flat.

"You're not taking her somewhere are you?" she asked, as Georgie lifted a suitcase onto the back seat of Judy's car.

"No, it's just some clothes I bought her. She lost her coat somewhere."

"I know. The police have got it."

Judy had looked up the address in her *A to Z* and soon found the right road.

"It's the top flat," said Georgie, as Judy parked

outside the red-brick house. "Are you sure you want to see her, Judy?"

Judy wasn't at all sure. "Perhaps it would be better if you went in alone," she said. "Seeing me might upset her. I'll wait in the car."

"All right," said Georgie. "I'll try not to be too long."

"Just be careful."

Judy watched Georgie mount the steps and ring the doorbell. The door opened and she went in. Judy looked at her watch. It was twenty-five to three. She decided that she would give Georgie thirty minutes before she started to worry, but that was easier said than done. There was no sound from the house, and the curtains in the top floor windows seemed to be closed.

Judy turned the car radio on for several minutes, then turned it off again. She looked at her watch. Only five minutes had passed. *This is stupid*, she thought. *I can't sit here worrying, I'll go for a walk.*

Judy got out of the car and walked to the end of the road. There was a small shop on the corner and she went in, wondering what she could buy from the little Pakistani man behind the counter. She returned to the car minutes later with a magazine and some cough sweets, just as Georgie came out of the house.

That was quick! Wasn't she there?"

"Oh yes, she's there, but she's very nervous," said Georgie. "I told her I was with a friend who would like to meet her."

"Oh no!" exclaimed Judy. "Does that mean I'll have to see her now?"

"Only if you want to. Of course, I had to persuade her that we hadn't brought the police, and that seemed to calm her down."

"Good, but before you go back in there, Georgie, I must ask you something. Do you know if she ever lived in Chicago?"

"Chicago? Not as far as I know. Her family had a big mansion somewhere near Boston, but her parents were killed in a car crash when she was ten."

"Oh," sighed Judy, as Georgie continued.

"But I did find out that she was adopted."

"What?" cried Judy. "Why did you do that?"

"After what you told me, Judy, I remembered that I had always wondered if she was adopted."

"Why?"

"Because I knew that her Jewish parents had come from Eastern Europe, and she is so fair, like you."

Judy stared at Georgie.

"Bloody Hell! I don't believe it. It can't be possible. Do you know where she was adopted? Could it have been in England?"

"That's something you'll have to ask her yourself. Judy, if you really want to know."

"Of course I want to know," said Judy.

"Well, come on then, you'd better come and meet her," said Georgie, taking her arm.

They had just stepped into the entrance hall of the house when they heard what they took to be the siren of an ambulance as it turned into the road, but as they turned to look, two police cars screeched to a halt behind Judy's car.

"Bloody Hell!" yelled Judy, grabbing hold of Georgie. "Quick! They mustn't find you here," she said, as she pushed Georgie down the hallway to a door at the rear. Luckily it was not locked, and they found themselves in a dark, musty kitchen.

"What are we going to do?" asked Georgie.

"We're going to get away from here," said Judy. "There must be a back entrance to the house."

"But your car... it's parked right outside," said Georgie.

"I know. Never mind about that," said Judy. "Here's the door," she whispered, as the sound of heavy footsteps pounded up the staircase above their heads.

The two girls found themselves in a narrow alleyway behind the houses. And moments later were back on the road some several hundred yards away from the house.

"Let's get up to the main road, and then we can find a taxi," said Judy.

"OK, but what about your car?" asked Georgie.

"That doesn't matter for the moment," said Judy. "I just wanted to get you away from there. You don't want the police to know you have been helping Suzanne, do you?"

"No, I certainly do not," agreed Georgie, "and I really am very grateful to you, Judy."

"Don't be silly," said Judy. "I don't want them to find me either, especially as I'm her double! And I wouldn't want to have to get the American embassy to rescue you. I can come back for the car later tonight."

There didn't seem to be any taxis about as they walked up the main road.

"I wonder how the police found out where she was?" remarked Judy. "Especially as you said she'd darkened her hair. How would anyone have recognised her?"

"Yes, I was wondering that," said Georgie. "Maybe it was the guy in the flat. He could have guessed who she was and called them."

They were just approaching the tube station, when two police cars came racing past them, their sirens screaming.

"Good grief! She must have got away!" cried Judy.

"Oh geez, now where's she gonna go?" moaned Georgie.

CHAPTER SEVENTEEN

"I've got a surprise for you, Jude," announced Bob one evening.

"Another?" asked Judy.

"We're going to France for the weekend."

"France! You must be psychic, darling," she cried. "I was going to ask you if you would like to come with me to see my Aunt Constance."

"Is that the aunt near Toulouse?"

"Yes."

"That's all right then; I've got the tickets. We're going on Friday evening."

"What, to Toulouse?"

"Of course. Henry wants to show us the farmhouse he's bought by the Canal du Midi."

"How super! I wonder if it's near Auntie."

"It's just outside Castelnaudary."

"Then I'll look it up on the map," said Judy.

Bob and Judy left Heathrow on the Air France flight the following Friday evening.

"You won't mind if I go to see Aunt Constance while we're there, will you, darling?" asked Judy.

"Of course not," he said. "It'll save you making another trip. But why now? You haven't seen her for years, have you?"

"I know, but I feel rather guilty, and with her seventy-fifth birthday coming up, I think I should see her, especially as she is alone now. Why don't you come with me? She was so pleased when I told her we were engaged."

"No, Judy, you go alone, but don't forget we've only got until Monday. Why don't you pop over on Sunday? You could take the hire car."

"All right, Bob. Thanks," she said.

On arrival at the clean, modern airport, Bob left Judy to wait for their suitcases while he joined the queue for a hire car, and thirty minutes later they were on the ring road leading to the autoroute in a new Peugeot 305. At well past midnight, the road seemed deserted, and they were soon halfway to Carcassonne, at the Castelnaudary exit.

"We have to get onto the D623," said Judy, studying the plan that Henry had sent. "It's the first turn off at the roundabout." Ten minutes later they were approaching the farmhouse on a drive flanked by huge poplar trees.

"Wow, it's huge!" exclaimed Judy, as they drove into the farmyard.

"Mmm, Henry's idea of a French country cottage, I suppose," remarked Bob, as he parked in front of the long Lauragais farmhouse. Henry stood grinning at the doorway in a pair of paint-stained jeans.

"So you made it!" he greeted them. "Come on in and have some wine."

Judy set off after lunch on Sunday in the hire car to see her Aunt Constance, promising to be back before dark. Constance lived about forty minutes away, in an eighteenth century maison de maître in the pretty village of St Felix-Lauragais. Unlike poor Mary, Judy's Aunt Constance was a very well preserved and still glamorous woman, and despite living in French farming countryside, surprised Judy, when she opened the door, immaculately dressed in a tailored trouser suit, her face carefully made-up.

"Auntie, you look marvellous!" exclaimed Judy, as she followed her into the large salon, where a log fire was lit.

"Come and sit over here by me, Judy," said Constance, as she beckoned to an antique chair by the Louis Fifteenth fireplace.

"This is cosy, and what a lot of work you've done!" remarked Judy, gazing around the room.

"Yes, I've been busy since Pierre died."

"I am sorry I wasn't able to come over to see you at the time. Mary wasn't well, and I had to find a new nursing home, but her condition is deteriorating now."

"I'm sorry," muttered Constance, sharply.

"I'm afraid I won't be able to stay for very long, Auntie," said Judy. "I had hoped to spend a weekend with you, but as Bob, my fiancé was invited over this weekend by a friend near Castelnaudary, I decided to come with him."

"That's all right, dear," said Constance. "Perhaps you can come with Bob another time. We'll have a chat and you can tell me all about him, then I'll show you the gardens before we have tea."

Judy had brought a file of old family photos with her, thinking that it would be a good way to get Constance to talk about the past, but it wasn't until they were sitting down to tea that Constance appeared relaxed.

There were several pictures of Judy's parents with Constance and Uncle Eric, the husband she had left, and after having talked about their old home in England, Judy managed to steer the conversation to a more personal level.

"I hope you don't mind my asking, Auntie, but why did you leave Eric?"

"Eric was a philanderer and a wastrel," announced Constance. "It was a pity that I didn't marry your father when I had the chance, but Mary took him off me."

"Really? I didn't know."

"I'd always known about his women, of course, but when he told me that his girlfriend was pregnant it was the last straw. I couldn't have any children, you see Judy," she said.

"Oh how awful. Poor you."

"The worst of it was that she was expecting twins, and when I heard that, I walked straight out."

"Twins! Gosh, they do run in the family, don't they?" remarked Judy.

"Why do you say that?"

"Well, you and Mummy are twins."

"We are fraternal twins, and we're not at all alike," said Constance, jumping up to refill Judy's teacup.

Judy wondered why her aunt seemed to be irritated at every mention of Mary.

"Did you know the girlfriend?" asked Judy.

"I thought I did, but I was mistaken," snapped Constance.

Judy had a sudden feeling that Constance knew all about her twin, but she still had no idea how she could approach the subject, until she realised that it was almost six o'clock and she had to get back to Castelnaudary.

As Judy prepared to leave, Constance asked, "What was it that you wanted to discuss with me, Judy? I almost forgot. I hope it doesn't concern Mary."

This is it, thought Judy, now I'll have to ask her.

"No, it's not Mary, Auntie, it's me."

"Oh? Not a problem with your fiancé, I hope?"

"No, there's no problem there. It concerns my birth, Auntie," she said, holding her breath.

"Your birth, Judy?" Constance's blue eyes stared at Judy.

"Yes, I believe you were there when I and my twin were born, were you not, Auntie?"

"You and your *what*?" cried Constance.

"Yes, me and my twin sister," said Judy. "She is alive, and I've seen her. In fact she killed somebody."

Constance swung round glaring at Judy. "What on earth are you talking about? What nonsense is this!"

"It's no good, Auntie, I know all about her."

"What absolute rubbish!" snapped Constance. "You *do not* have a sister, Judy, and never have had. And now I think you had better leave before you anger me any further."

"I'm sorry, but I had to ask you." Judy felt herself blushing at her aunt's outburst.

"You haven't asked me anything, Judy," snapped Constance. "You simply made a ridiculous and completely unfounded statement."

"It was not unfounded, Auntie. I've seen the hospital records of our birth, and I believe that my twin sister may have been adopted."

"What?" yelled Constance, now quite red in the face. "I think you'd better go, Judy!"

During the flight home the following day, Judy thought back to her aunt's anger, and all that she had said, and new suspicions began to dawn in her mind. It seemed obvious that Constance knew that Mary had given birth to twins, but what had happened to the other baby, whether she was dead or alive, remained a mystery. Constance may not know any more. But why had she seemed so offhand when Judy mentioned Mary? Was the reason that they quarrelled because Mary had married the man that Constance wanted? Of had her refusal to even consider the existence of Judy's twin revealed another family secret?

Judy pulled the file of photos out from her bag, and laid them on the plastic tray in front of her. She picked up the pictures showing the two couples together remembering how, when she was young, everybody remarked how like her uncle she was. Peering at Eric's face, she realised that there was no denying the resemblance, and worse, how unlike her beloved father she was.

"Bloody Hell!" exclaimed Judy, her heart beating wildly. "No wonder Constance was so angry, and no wonder she left Eric!"

"What are you talking about, Jude?" asked Bob, disturbed from his financial pages.

"Daddy wasn't my father!" she announced.

"What? Now what are you on about, Judy? Don't tell me you're onto that twin thing again. Is that why you wanted to see your aunt? Have you upset her?"

"I tried not to."

"But what's this about your father, Judy? Did she tell you something?"

"I think she did. Look at these photos, Bob," she

said, pointing to her uncle's face. "Do you see any resemblance?"

"With what?" he asked.

"With me."

"Yes, you are quite like him, Judy, but that's not unusual. He was your uncle."

"Now look at my father," said Judy. "Do I look like him?"

Bob frowned as he peered down at the picture. "What are you getting at, Judy?"

"Can't you see, darling? Constance was in love with Daddy, but he married Mary instead, so she married Eric, the philanderer. But when his girlfriend fell pregnant, she left him."

"So? How does this affect you, Judy?"

"Eric's girlfriend was expecting twins, and I think it was Mary."

"Mary? Do you mean your mother?"

"Exactly. Now do you understand?"

Bob laid down his newspaper and turned to Judy. "Well, that's some story, Judy. Are you sure you're not letting your imagination run amok?"

"No, I'm not. I know I promised to forget all about the twin, darling, but I've been thinking about it for ages, and now everything seems to be fitting into place."

"So are you saying that your mother had an affair with Eric, and that he fathered you and the dead twin?"

"That's right."

"Do you have any proof?"

"No, but if you'd seen the way Auntie reacted, you'd understand, and I have seen the hospital records of our birth, which proves that mummy did have twins."

"Oh my God!" was all that Bob could say.

"Look. Judy," said Bob, as the hostess took away their lunch trays. "Could we postpone any further discussion about your family until we get home? We've had a lovely relaxing weekend with Henry, and I don't think I can take any more of your chromosomal fantasies."

"But I'm not fantasising, Bob. I *did* have a twin sister!"

"Yes, yes I know. But can we just leave it at that, Judy? Why don't you finish that book you brought with you? You're not doing yourself any favours by continuing to poke into your family's murky past." Bob was sounding quite annoyed.

"I'm sorry, darling. I shouldn't have bothered you with it. You're quite right of course," said Judy, pulling a paperback from her bag. Oh Lord, I think I've gone too far. I should never have let him know what I was doing.

Judy returned to her flat alone that evening to find a message on her answerphone. It was from Georgie, telling her she was returning to New York that day, and reminding Judy to email her if there was any news of Suzanne.

Judy lay awake that night, trying to picture her mother with Eric.

It can't be true! Mummy would never have been unfaithful to Daddy, she told herself, remembering the loving relationship of her parents. She knew that her father had been away quite frequently on business when she was young, so could something have happened then? But Mary was shy and old-fashioned, as well as being nearly always ill, so what on earth would the licentious Eric have seen in her? And what about poor Daddy? If something had happened with Eric, had he known about it? Judy started to weep into her pillow. She had adored her kind-hearted father. She didn't want Eric as her father. It just didn't make sense.

"When are we getting married, Jude?" asked Bob, as they lay in bed one Sunday morning, some weeks later.

"Tomorrow, if you like, darling. I could wear that lovely suit you bought me."

"I wish we could, but there is the slight problem of the licence; which reminds me…"

"What?"

"Can you get a bit of time off work next week?"

"I don't know. Perhaps. But what for?"

"A friend of mine has several nice properties lined up for us to see," said Bob.

"Properties?" exclaimed Judy, sitting up, surprised.

"All right – houses. I've been thinking, Judy, since we saw that lovely place of Henry's, that we could do something similar."

"Do you mean that you want us to go and live in France?"

"No, not immediately. But as property prices have risen so sharply in that part of France, it would be foolish to wait," said Bob. "I think we should go for a smallish house here to start with, and invest in something over there for our retirement."

"But darling, you're talking about a huge investment!" objected Judy. "And you know I've got hardly any savings."

"I can afford it, Judy; and even if I did retire from the firm early, I could continue working consensually in France."

"Gosh! It sounds wonderful, darling, but I hadn't realised that I would be marrying a millionaire!"

Bob laughed, as he pulled her back beside him. "I'm certainly not that, Judy, but I've worked hard to get where I am, and I consider myself very lucky to have a wonderful girl like you to share my rewards."

"Oh Bob, I love you so much!" cried Judy. "I don't care where we live as long as I'm with you, and I'll never let you down, I promise."

"I know that you won't, Gorgeous, and I'm just so pleased that you've finally put all that twin business behind you. I was worried there for a while. You were becoming almost obsessed."

After a quick brunch, Bob drove Judy out of London to explore some of the villages north of Salisbury. Judy agreed that she would be more than happy to base herself somewhere between Salisbury and Winchester, a part of the country that both she and Bob were fond of, and on the way home that evening they decided to marry in September.

CHAPTER EIGHTEEN

It had been raining almost nonstop for weeks, and the Easter weekend had been a complete washout. It would soon be Whitsun, and Bob and Judy had tired of scouring the boggy countryside in torrential rain, trudging round unsuitable pseudo-period homes.

"We're never going to find anything," moaned Judy, curled up on the sofa watching television one wet Sunday afternoon. "At this rate there won't be time to do any decorating before we move in!"

"Cheer up, gorgeous," laughed Bob. "We'll find something next week, I've got a feeling."

Judy met Pat for lunch the next day in an Italian restaurant.

"I feel like a lasagne and some red wine," said Judy. "I'm fed up with this B-awful weather, and all my shoes are caked with mud."

"So you haven't found your dream home yet then?" asked Pat.

"What do you think? It's been a total waste of time so far, and we're lucky we haven't caught pneumonia."

"How is Bob coping?"

"Oh, he's as cool as ever. Nothing seems to worry

him."

"Not even you?"

"I hope not."

The restaurant was filling up quickly and as the waitress left with their order, two tall men in dark suits sat down at the table behind them.

"There's no hurry, is there? You're not getting married till September," said Pat. "If you start panicking now, goodness knows what you'll be like when you walk up the aisle."

"Into the Registry Office! We're not having a big wedding; just a few friends afterwards. Bob's parents are dead, and I don't have any family who could come."

"And definitely no twin sister, thank God," added Pat, as one of the men at the table turned sharply around.

"I thought I recognised your voice," said the tall man as he stood up to face Judy.

"Inspector McGregor!"

"How are you, Miss Hay?"

"I'm very well," she replied, turning to Pat. "This is the inspector in charge of the stabbing on the tube."

"Oh not that again!" murmured Pat. "Did you catch the murderer, Inspector?"

"We are still pursuing our enquiries," he replied.

Judy's heart missed a beat, remembering the police cars racing up the road after Suzanne's escape from the house.

"You must have questioned a number of suspects, apart from me, Inspector. Have you not made any arrests?"

"No, Miss Hay. Our main suspect seems to have disappeared from the face of the earth."

"Oh, I'm sorry," mumbled Judy, as their pasta

arrived, and McGregor returned to his table.

"Is that the policeman who hauled you in for questioning?" whispered Pat.

"One of them, and if I hadn't met Jean, they'd have arrested me too."

"Well, thank goodness he seems to have forgotten about that now, and you too, Judy," remarked Pat, as she reached for the carafe of wine.

Judy was alone in the office the next day. London was very quiet after Easter, and John was still away with his family in the Algarve. Judy was bored, and as there seemed to be no new orders coming their way, she spent most of the day chucking out old correspondence files and studying the new entries in the manufacturers' directory. By lunchtime on Wednesday, having spent most of the morning drawing plans for her ideal country home, her mind began to wander back to Suzanne and to what Georgie had told her, when an idea suddenly flashed through her head.

Is it possible that my twin could have been taken away for adoption without either my parents or Constance knowing? And if she was adopted, and Suzanne, who looks exactly like me was adopted, then Suzanne *must* be my twin!

Judy decided to return to the hospital. Where else could she find out what had happened? *There's got to be somebody there who knows, or perhaps there's an adoption agency in Winchester*, she thought, as she drove out of London that afternoon.

Judy parked in the hospital car park and walked slowly towards the main entrance. She couldn't think where she should go. Would it be the Almoner who handled adoptions from the hospital, or should she try the maternity clinic again? Then she thought of the Personnel Department. With a bit of luck they might still hold the nursing records for 1952.

The waiting room was full of people, and as Judy sat trying to work out what she should say, a woman appeared at the reception desk to tell her that the office for nursing staff was down the corridor. Judy sat down to wait again in a smaller room with several young women, wondering if she should pretend she was looking for a job. The interviews were being held in an inner office, and each applicant seemed to be in there for ages. After a while, a smartly-dressed woman with silver hair came in and told the girl on reception desk to go for her tea break. She put on her reading glasses and glanced across at Judy.

"Are you here for an interview?" she asked.

"No, I'm sorry, I'm not here for a job. I was just hoping to make some enquiries."

"I thought you didn't look like a nurse," said the woman.

Judy smiled, wondering how she should have looked. She stood up and walked over to the desk.

"I am hoping that someone can help me. You see I was born here, in Winchester General Hospital in nineteen fifty-two."

"Oh yes? I was here then," remarked the woman.

Judy stared.

"Were you really? Were you a nurse?"

"No, I was a ward secretary, on the surgical ward, but I'm retired now. I come here two days a week to help out. But what can I do for you, my dear?"

"I was hoping to find someone who was in the

maternity ward when I was born, and I wondered if there may still be records of the nursing staff held here."

"Oh dear, I shouldn't think so, it's over thirty years ago!"

"I know," sighed Judy despondently, "but I thought it was worth a try. Do you think they would be with the archives at the County Records Office?"

"I've no idea," replied the woman. "Perhaps if you could tell me exactly what you are looking for, I'll see if I can help."

Then Judy described what she had found at the Records Office, and her suspicions that her twin may have been taken away for adoption.

"My goodness, how extraordinary!" remarked the older woman when Judy had finished. "There is something familiar about your story, my dear. Give me your birth date and your mother's name. I think I just may be able to help you."

"Really? That's wonderful!" exclaimed Judy, as she hastily scribbled down her name and details of her birth on a piece of paper.

"My name is Anne Browning, and I'll give you my phone number," said the kind woman. "I can't promise to come up with anything, Judy, but I do have an old friend who was a midwife here, and she may be able to help."

"A midwife?" cried Judy. "Does she live in Winchester?"

"No, my dear, she's in London, but we keep in touch regularly. I'll have a word with her, and if you will telephone me in a few days, I'll let you know if she can help."

"Oh, thank you so much, Mrs Browning. It will be such a relief if I can find out what happened to my sister."

Driving back to London, Judy's confidence that she may soon learn what had happened quickly faded when the possibility of a secret adoption with its myriad complexities forced its way uppermost into her mind. If Suzanne was adopted, why is she American and not English? How could a baby born in England end up in America? And if it was true, who arranged it? It wasn't her father, because it was he who registered the baby's death. Then she thought of Aunt Constance. How she must have hated Mary! But even that made no sense, because she would surely have taken the baby for herself. And did Mary breakdown because she was told the baby was dead, or could it have been because she found out that it had been taken away alive?

The next day seemed to go on for ever to Judy. All afternoon she kept looking at the telephone, longing to call Anne Browning to see if she had spoken to the midwife, but she knew that she must wait at least a couple of days.

On Thursday afternoon, however, she decided to call her, only to hear that there had been no reply to the midwife's number, and that Anne would try again that evening.

Judy finished the washing-up and walked back into the living room. It was Friday evening, and she was missing Bob. He had been away in Manchester and had promised to call her as soon as he got back on Saturday. She had just picked up the telephone to call Anne Browning, when she heard a scuffling noise outside her door, then a key turning in the lock. Startled, she dropped the receiver and turned to find Bob struggling through the doorway half hidden by an enormous parcel.

"Bob!" she cried. "What a surprise. I didn't think you were coming back until tomorrow."

"Well, if that's the welcome I get, I'll go away again," he replied, dropping the heavy, brown paper-covered parcel to the floor.

"Come here, silly," she said, throwing her arms around him.

"That's better," laughed Bob, as he lifted her up and carried her over to the sofa.

"Now will you tell me?" asked Judy, after she had unravelled herself from his embraces.

"Tell you what?"

"The parcel; what is it?"

"It's for our house. I picked it up at a sale in Manchester. My client took me to an auction."

"Ah, so that's what you get up to when you're away on business, is it?" Now it was Judy's turn to tease.

Bob snorted pulling her roughly to the floor.

"We'll have to cut the string," she said, freeing herself.

"It's a Turkish rug," announced Bob.

"A Turkish rug! It must have cost a fortune, darling."

"I'll have nothing but the best for my little wife," said Bob. "But tell me, Gorgeous, what have you been up to?"

"Nothing," said Judy blushing. "Nothing at all. It's dead at work, and I'm bored to tears."

"Then the sooner we get you settled down in the country, the better."

"Oh Bob!" sighed Judy. "I can't wait to have your babies."

That weekend they found the house. It was a late eighteenth century, red-brick parsonage on the edge of a small village, a few miles east of Salisbury. Judy had fallen in love with it even before the estate agent had unlocked the door, and Bob, too, was delighted. The overgrown garden at the rear was full of flowering shrubs, Hollyhocks and roses, and behind that lay a small orchard.

"You don't feel it may be a little too quiet for you, Judy?" Bob had asked.

"Oh no," she'd cried. "If we live here, darling, I'll never go out."

Judy was so excited about the house when she got to work the next morning, that she had totally forgotten about her missing twin when she picked up the phone to tell Pat her news. It was not until later that afternoon that she remembered to call Anne Browning in Winchester.

"Oh, Miss Hay, I'm sorry, but I don't yet have anything to tell you," said the kind woman.

"Oh dear," sighed Judy, suddenly deflated.

"I rang my friend's number several times, and finally someone else answered her phone. I'm afraid my friend is in hospital."

"Oh no," exclaimed Judy, unable to hide her disappointment.

"She had a fall last week, so she may be in hospital for some time. I am sorry to disappoint you, Judy, but I'll try to get to see her as soon as she is well enough."

"I hope she isn't badly hurt."

"I believe she had broken her arm, so it could have been worse, although the shock doesn't help at her age."

"I really do appreciate your trying to help me,

Anne," said Judy. "I'll wait until I hear from you, shall I?"

"Of course, my dear. I will telephone you as soon as I have spoken to her."

"Well, that's that then," muttered Judy to herself, after she had hung up. "Perhaps now I'll never know what happened."

Bob's offer for the pretty house was accepted the following week, and he and Judy would take possession in July.

CHAPTER NINETEEN

When the phone rang in Judy's office two days later, she was surprised to hear the heavy accent of Detective Sergeant Jones.

"We would like you to call in at the station some time today, Miss Hay, if you don't mind."

"Oh no! Whatever for, Sergeant?"

"It'll only take a few minutes, Miss. We need your help with an identification."

Judy's heart jumped. Did it mean that they had arrested Suzanne, and wanted her to identify her? She imagined herself struggling to pick out the wrong woman in a line-up of policewomen.

"Have you made an arrest, Sergeant?" she asked.

"Not yet, but we want you to take a look at something," he said.

"Something?"

"Could you call by after lunch, Miss Hay?"

Hell! thought Judy. "Yes, I suppose I could if you think it's really necessary."

"Good," said Jones. "We will expect you at about two thirty then."

Judy rang Bob at his office.

"What do you think they want?" she asked.

"I've no idea," said Bob. "Perhaps they have found something belonging to that woman."

"It could be her coat; perhaps they think I will remember it."

"I shouldn't worry about it, Judy. You must just help them in any way you can now."

When Judy arrived at the police station, she was greeted by Detective Constable Leary.

"We'd like you to look at something, Miss," he said, as he offered her a chair.

Judy felt suddenly nervous. What if it was a body? What if Suzanne had killed someone else?

"I don't know why you think I can help," she remarked.

"We've already shown it to the doctor," said Leary, as he opened up a file and pulled out a picture. "And as you were standing near the victim, and stated that you had seen the suspect, we are hoping that you will be able to identify the person in this picture."

Judy stared at the image of her double that he had placed in front of her. "Where did you get this?"

"It came in from the States this morning," replied Detective Sergeant Jones, as he walked over to them.

"The States?"

"Yes, from the Illinois CIA, to be precise."

"Illinois? Chicago, Illinois?" asked Judy, her heart pounding.

"Correct," said Jones. "What do you know about that, Miss Hay?"

"Only what the victim's girlfriend told me. But this is incredible!"

"Is something worrying you, Miss Hay?" asked

Leary, aware of Judy's unease.

"Before we go any further," interrupted Jones, "I want you to tell me if you have ever seen this woman, Miss Hay. Can you positively identify this picture as being an exact likeness of the woman you saw on the tube train on Thursday, December the third last year."

Judy took a deep breath. "I'm not sure. It does look similar to the picture in the paper."

"That doesn't answer my question. I want to know if you have ever seen the woman in the photo either before, during or after the incident on the tube."

Judy began to feel hot. What was he getting at?

"I suppose it could be the same woman, but it's not very clear, is it?" she said, peering at the computerised image before her. "Is it an actual photograph, or is it one of those made up pictures you put together?"

"Just answer the question, Miss Hay."

"Well, it could be the woman I saw at Victoria, and it's not unlike me either, is it?"

"Our thoughts precisely," said Jones.

"Well, I can't see how that helps you," said Judy. "You've always known that the woman in the red coat looks like me. And for your information, Sergeant, I have *never* been to Chicago. May I go now?"

Judy stood up to leave. She had had enough of their questioning.

"Oh, by the way, Miss Hay," said Jones, as she reached the door. "We do know that you were an only child."

Judy turned furiously towards the policeman. "Are you saying that you have been poking about into my family? I want to see Inspector McGregor!"

"The Chief Inspector is not on the premises," said

Jones.

We'll see about that! thought Judy, as she walked out.

"She's hiding something," remarked Leary.

"I agree. I think we'd better keep an eye on Miss Hay."

Judy's legs were shaking when she reached the lift on the second floor. As the door opened, a smartly-dressed young policewoman stepped out.

"Can you help me?" Judy asked. "I'm looking for Chief Inspector McGregor's office."

"You're on the wrong floor. Is he expecting you?"

"Oh yes!" lied Judy.

"It's the next floor up, the second door on the left," said the smiling girl.

"Thank you," said Judy, stepping smartly into the lift.

Half an hour later Judy had told the inspector all about her feelings on seeing her double on the tube, and her hunch that she may have a twin sister.

"Why are you telling me this?" McGregor wanted to know.

"Because I hoped that you would understand why I may have appeared to be uncooperative."

"You were."

"I just couldn't help believing that she was my twin, even though I had always been told that I was an only child, and that's why I had to find out for myself."

"Go on," said McGregor.

"I went to St Catherine's House to check my birth registration, Inspector, and there is no doubt that I am my mother's only child. I can show you a copy of my birth certificate, if you like."

"Detective Sergeant Jones has already verified that, Miss Hay, so I don't really know why you came to see me."

"I am here, Chief Inspector, because I don't like being harassed by your sergeant."

"You are not being harassed by anyone, Miss Hay. Have you forgotten that this is a murder enquiry?"

"No, of course not, as if I could," said Judy.

"Then perhaps you would be good enough to allow us to continue with our investigations? Good day, Miss Hay."

Judy left the building feeling like a naughty child, unsure whether or not she had been wise to tell McGregor anything at all. What if she had given him the impression that she was still holding something back? And what if they had seen the death registration of her twin? Could they haul her back for not telling them about that? *Oh Lord, I think I've put my foot in it,* she thought.

Judy's boss had been delighted with the news of her engagement, despite knowing that, as the wife of a successful lawyer, she would hardly want to spend her days rustling up trading contracts, so he was not surprised when she told him she would like to leave at the end of June. John had been thinking of retiring for some time, and his Kuwaiti partners were ready to take over the London office.

Some weeks were to pass before Judy was to hear again from the kind lady at the hospital in Manchester, and she had barely given a thought to the mystery of her twin. Her head had been full of the pretty house that was to be her future home, and she and Bob had been down to

Wiltshire a couple of times to check what work needed to be done before they moved in.

Anne Browning had spent a week in London helping her friend, the retired midwife, and on her return home, she had phoned Judy.

"As soon as I had finished relating your story to her," she told Judy, "she immediately remembered the day when your mother lost her baby, and when I expressed my surprise, she told me it was because of the scandal."

"The scandal?"

"Exactly, and then I realised why I had thought there was something familiar about your story, because it had been there at the back of my memory too."

"But what scandal? Was it something to do with my mother?"

"Oh no, my dear; not directly."

Judy's head was in whirl. What on earth was she going to hear now?

"Judy, I think it would be better if you could come to see me. This really is not something that I care to tell you over the phone."

"Oh, but I can't, I'm too busy," moaned Judy. "Can't you tell me what it is now?"

Ten minutes later, Judy was sitting stunned at her desk, scarcely able to believe that her baby sister may have been stolen from the hospital. But if someone had taken her twin, did it mean that they must have revived her after she had been declared dead? And how could that be possible? But there was no certainty that that was what had happened to Judy's sister.

All that Anne had told her was that, soon after Judy's birth, a nurse at the hospital had been arrested for her involvement in a racket supplying newly born English babies to an illegal adoption agency in America.

"What's the matter, Gorgeous? Can't you sleep?" asked Bob, as Judy tossed and turned in bed that night. "You've woken me up again."

"I'm sorry, Darling," said Judy, turning towards him. "It's no good, I'll have to get up."

"It's three o'clock in the morning! Is something worrying you?"

"Not really, I just can't get off. I'm so excited about the house and everything." How could she tell him now that she was certain that Suzanne really was her twin? I just can't, she told herself, as she threw off the duvet and rolled out of bed.

"Judy! Come here," moaned Bob, pulling the duvet back.

"I'm going to make a cup of cocoa. Go back to sleep, darling. I won't disturb you again, I promise."

A week later, Judy was knocking on the door of a flat on the third floor of a block of council flats in East London. She had found the address of the retired midwife in the telephone directory some days earlier, and now as she waited, she suddenly found herself wondering what she was doing there.

Anne Browning has insisted that she had told Judy all that her friend remembered about the scandal of the stolen babies, so what could she tell her now? And what right did Judy have to disturb the old nurse with something that happened thirty-eight years ago? I'm a selfish idiot. I should never have come, she told herself, as a wave of embarrassment caused her to turn away. She was just leaving, when she heard a door opening behind her.

"Hello? Is someone there?" she heard, and blushing, turned to see a grey-haired lady peering round the doorway.

Judy spent an enjoyable afternoon chatting with the elderly lady, who hadn't seemed at all put out by Judy's unexpected arrival. She had been on duty at Winchester Hospital at the time of Judy's birth, and she had remembered the day when a mother had given birth to a stillborn twin, because of the panic afterwards. She told Judy that when her hysterical mother had insisted on seeing the dead baby, it had already been removed from the delivery ward, and there had been a terrible commotion when they couldn't find it. Its tiny body had completely disappeared from the hospital. It was not until some weeks later that the nurse had been arrested, and the scandal over the stolen babies came to light.

"If my mother had found out that someone had stolen the baby, that would explain her breakdown, wouldn't it?" Judy asked.

"Most probably," agreed the midwife.

"Do you think that is what happened to my twin?"

"It hardly seems likely."

"But not impossible? I mean, would it be possible to resuscitate a stillborn baby?"

"New born babies are resuscitated every day, but you say that your twin was registered as dead?"

"Yes, she was. But who would have said that she was dead? Surely it had to be a doctor?"

"It should be, of course; but if none was available, then the ward sister or the midwife would be responsible."

"So do you think that someone could have made a mistake?"

"There is always that possibility," was the reply.

The old midwife was unable to tell Judy anything more. She couldn't remember the name of the nurse who was arrested, but there had been a lot of publicity over the trial, and the nurse was sent to prison. Before Judy left, she promised that she would try to remember the names of the nurses who were on the maternity ward at the time.

Judy returned home, her head spinning. How on earth would she be able to find out if her twin really had been one of the stolen babies?

The midwife had said that there had been a trial, and the nurse sent to prison. That meant that the police must hold the records, but how could she go back to Inspector McGregor now that she had told him that she *didn't* have a twin? Then she thought of the newspapers. If she could find the report of the trial, it would surely give the nurse's name. And perhaps also something about the contacts in America.

"Where have you been, gorgeous?" asked Bob, as she walked into the kitchen where he was standing chopping vegetables. "You haven't been spending all your credit at Harvey Nichols, have you?"

"Certainly not! Although I did find some super curtain material at Liberty's the other day. I had tea with a friend from the office. But what are you making, darling?"

"I thought I'd have a go at a chicken and vegetable couscous."

"Ooh lovely! I don't feel much like cooking tonight."

"You look tired, Jude."

"Yes, I am a bit," she said. Hoping that he couldn't read her mind as well as he read her face. "I think I'll have a shower."

"You just relax, gorgeous. I'll take care of dinner."

"Oh Bob, you are wonderful!"

"I know," he laughed.

CHAPTER TWENTY

When Judy arrived at work on Monday morning, she immediately phoned Pat.

"I think I'll burst if I don't talk to someone soon," she said.

"Why? What's happened?"

"Nothing's happened. It's just that I need some advice. I don't know what to do next," replied Judy.

"Whatever is it? Is it Bob?" Pat sounded concerned.

"No, of course not; but listen Pat, I'm pretty sure now that Suzanne is my twin."

"Oh no! You've not been worrying about that again, have you?"

"Please Pat, just meet me for lunch, and I'll tell you all about it."

When Judy arrived at the Italian restaurant in Albemarle Street, Pat was waiting, grim-faced at the table they had occupied before. She had barely sat down before Pat began to scold her.

"Oh Judy, why can't you leave it alone? You know that woman's a murderer, so what good will it do to go poking about into her life? I don't understand you sometimes. You've got everything going for you, and yet you seem determined to continue with this crazy twin idea. Surely you realise how you could be antagonising Bob? You could even lose him!"

"Oh no, he'd never leave me over that."

"I wouldn't be so sure. Now, just tell me exactly what you've found out, Judy."

Thirty minutes later, Pat had hardly touched her meal, as she sat silently absorbing Judy's account of her meeting with Georgie, her research at Winchester, her visit to her aunt, and her afternoon with the retired midwife.

"Is that it?" she asked, when Judy had finished.

"Isn't it enough?"

Pat sighed heavily. "Look, Judy, I just don't know what to say to you, and I don't understand why you haven't confided in Bob."

"I just can't," said Judy. "He thinks I've forgotten all about it, and he'd be so angry."

"So what? It wouldn't be the end of the world, would it? In any case, you'll have to go to the police if you really want to know if your twin was one of the stolen babies. Either that or forget her. There's no other way."

"But how can I when I've only just told Inspector McGregor that I was an only child?"

"Oh Judy, for heaven's sake, you'll have to make your mind up. Either you want to find out if your twin was taken to America, or you don't!"

"I know you're right, Pat, but it's so difficult."

"Just do it," said Pat, squeezing Judy's hand. "Now, could we change the subject?"

"All right. I'm sorry to be such a bore," said Judy.

As they waited for their coffee, Judy leant across the table towards Pat. "Don't turn around," she whispered, "but there's a man over there who keeps looking at us."

"A man? What sort of man?"

"An ordinary, clean-looking man, I suppose, but he looks sort of cagey. I think he's following me. I'm sure he was on the tube this morning."

"Oh, come on now, Judy, you must be imagining it."

"No, I'm not. Oh Lord! He's looking over here again. Do you think he could be a policeman?"

"Why on earth would a policeman be following you, Judy?"

"Because I think they suspect me again."

"What? Of killing that man?"

"Perhaps, or maybe they think I know something. I told you I had to go back to the police station again, didn't I?"

"Yes, but surely they're not going to waste their time trailing innocent people. Look Judy, I told you to go to the police if you want to get to the bottom of all this, so just do it!

"Why don't you go and ask that man who he is, if you really thing he's following you? I'm sure he'll tell you if he is a policeman, and if he's some crank, he'll probably just run away."

"All right, I'll do it," said Judy.

As the girls left their table, the man sitting on the opposite side of the restaurant stood up and walked smartly towards the exit.

"Quick!" whispered Pat. "Go and ask him. I'll get the bill," she added, pushing Judy ahead of her.

Judy grabbed her bag and hurried across the room.

"Damn!" she muttered, startling the girl at the cash desk, as the man left. She hesitated for a second, glancing back towards Pat.

"My friend's paying," she told the girl, as she pulled

open the door and rushed out into the street.

Judy looked quickly down the road, straining to recognise the man's back among the people going towards Piccadilly, before wheeling round to scan the top end of the road, but she couldn't see the man.

"Look! He's over on the other side!" said Pat, pointing across the road.

"Where?" asked Judy, dashing straight into the path of a speeding taxi.

"What the Hell...!" yelled the driver, leaning shocked out of his cab.

"Judy!" screamed Pat, grabbing her arm to pull her across to the other side of the road.

"Well, you told me to go after him. Where is he?"

"I don't know. Perhaps we'd better forget it," replied her shaken friend.

When Judy arrived at her office on Friday, she found an email from Georgie, asking if she had any news about Suzanne. She remembered that Georgie had given Suzanne a train ticket for Scotland, and wondered if she could have flown back to New York from there. She replied that the police were still looking for Suzanne, and that she would write with news of all that she had discovered.

It was the twenty-ninth of June and Judy's last day at work, and a steady stream of well-wishers called in to say goodbye. There were over a hundred people working for several different companies in the building, and Judy was surprised at the number of cards she received. An enormous tropical plant from Madeira appeared on her desk from the boys in the shipping office upstairs, and the three girls in the tour operator's office below arrived with a large box of saucepans.

John took Judy out for lunch at a favourite Greek restaurant, and by four o'clock, her office was littered with plastic mugs and torn wrapping paper.

As John said goodbye to Judy, he handed her an envelope containing a card. On it was a picture of a lawn mower, with a telephone number written underneath. Judy glanced up at John, puzzled.

"As soon as you're settled, Ducky, you call this number and they'll deliver it," he said.

"What?" she asked.

"It's an electric one for your garden, Judy. You never did let the grass grow under your feet, did you?"

"Oh, John, not a lawn mower? What a wonderful wedding present!" she cried. Inside the card was a picture of a pram, and underneath John had written: 'Don't leave it too long!' Judy threw her arms around him, tears springing from her laughing eyes.

"You'll be our first guest to dinner, John, I promise, and you must be our first child's godfather."

CHAPTER TWENTY-ONE

Bob and Judy set off for the Surrey nursing home to see Judy's mother. It had been several weeks since Judy's last visit, and she was feeling rather guilty. Bob had been with her before, but this time they planned to tell Mary that they would soon be getting married.

"I'll go and see the doctor, while you talk to your mother," said Bob, as he parked the car.

"But you will come and see her, won't you, darling?" asked Judy. "It may be the last time."

"Of course I will," he said.

Judy knocked on the door of her mother's room, and went in. Mary was lying, fully dressed on her bed as a nurse stood taking her pulse. Judy nodded silently to the nurse.

"How is she?" she whispered.

The nurse glanced up from her watch, shaking her head.

"She's not been too good these last few days," she replied, as Mary's eyes flickered open. "I wouldn't stay too long if I were you," she added, as she left the room.

Judy moved a chair nearer to the bed and sat down to take Mary's hand.

"Hello, Mummy. It's me, Judy."

"Judy?"

Judy bent down to kiss her.

"Judy?" said Mary again.

Judy longed to tell her mother what she had found out about the stolen babies, but she knew that she mustn't upset her. On the other hand, was it possible that hearing that her lost baby was alive could help to stall Mary's decline into oblivion? Perhaps the news might at least bring her a moment of joy? But, remembering Bob's scolding, she decided to say nothing about it.

"Mummy, I have brought someone else to see you today," said Judy, as she helped Mary to drink her tea; Mary's blue eyes looked vaguely up at Judy. "Bob came with me today, Mummy."

"Bob, bob, bob, bob…" muttered Mary, turning her face into the pillow.

"We're going to be married soon, Mummy," Judy continued, but there seemed to be no response. "Can you hear me, Mummy? It's me, Judy."

But Mary wasn't able to understand anything that Judy said. Judy squeezed Mary's hand. *Perhaps it would be better not to try to talk*, she thought, hoping that Mary would at least know that she was there.

Judy turned round and switched on the radio by Mary's bed, wondering if perhaps some music would help.

There was a knock on the door.

"Hello! How is she?" asked Bob as he walked over towards the bed.

"Not good," whispered Judy. "Look, Mummy, here's your other visitor."

"Hello, Mary, you look very cosy there," said Bob, pulling up a chair to the other side of the bed.

Mary blinked, turning her head sharply towards him. "Eric!" she cried, suddenly springing into life, her arms reaching out towards Bob.

"Bloody Hell!" muttered Judy. "No, Mummy, it's Bob. We're going to be married soon."

"Yes, Mary, I'm going to marry Judy in September."

"And I'll be able to come and see you much more often," added Judy, hopefully.

"Marry Eric? Where is he?" asked Mary, struggling to sit up in the bed. Judy glanced helplessly over towards Bob.

"It's me, Bob," he said, taking hold of Mary's other hand. "I'm going to marry Judy, and we'll bring you a piece of wedding cake, won't we, Judy?"

"Oh, for heaven's sake, it's no good," whispered Judy, despairingly, as the nurse returned.

"How are you getting on?" she enquired.

"Not very well, I'm afraid," replied Bob. "I think we had better leave now, don't you, Judy?"

Judy shook her head. She wanted to stay longer. There must be a way she could get through to her mother. She didn't want to leave her like that. She may not have another chance to talk to her. But it was useless.

As they drove silently away from the nursing home, tears began to trickle down Judy's face. Although she had never been close to her mother, it was scarcely bearable to see her like that.

"Well, that wasn't much fun, was it, darling?" remarked Bob. "And what was that about Eric?"

"I don't know, and I don't care," snapped Judy.

Bob turned sharply towards her.

"I'm sorry, Judy; I can see you are upset. But you did your best, and I'm sure she knew you were there.

That's what counts, isn't it?"

"Is it? If only I could talk to her, Bob. I feel so guilty."

"You've nothing to feel guilty about, Judy. Remember you sold your inheritance to pay for the nursing home, and your mother is being well looked after. There is nothing more that you can do. Let's just go home and try not to think about it. You must show me the colour scheme you've chosen for our bedroom."

"You're right, darling. I'm sorry."

Several days later, Mary Hay died in her sleep.

Judy hadn't seen much of her friends since leaving her job, but despite being fully occupied with preparations for the move into her new home, she persuaded Bob that she must devote one Saturday to visiting her friend, Sandy.

Sandy had invited Judy to lunch so, after stopping at Marks & Spencer to pick up a fruit flan, she caught a bus up the Edgware Road.

Sandy's flat was in a small block off Kendal Street, and when Judy got off the bus, she knew that she was being followed. *Oh why can't they leave me alone!* she moaned inwardly, feeling certain that it must be the police.

She hesitated for a moment before darting into a nearby chemist shop. There was a queue of people waiting to be served, and not sure what she could buy, Judy busied herself studying the display of homeopathic medicine, glancing occasionally through the windows to see if there was anyone hanging around outside. *This is silly*, she thought. *Sandy will wonder where I am*. And she hurried back out into the street.

Judy had just turned the corner into Kendal Street, when she saw a smartly-dressed dark-haired woman hurrying out of the main entrance of the famous Park West block of flats on the other side of the road. Judy stared across the road for several moments, unable to move, as a shock wave passed through her head.

Bloody Hell! It can't be! She *can't* still be in London! But there was no doubt in Judy's mind. It was her twin! She wanted to rush over to her, to tell her who she was, and that she would help her, but she couldn't move. Her legs had turned to jelly and her feet felt glued to the ground. She had never felt so gutless in her life.

Suzanne was looking up and down the road for a taxi.

Oh God, I'm going to lose her, thought Judy, as she stood, her heart beating a hole through her ribs. Then Suzanne turned her head and their eyes met.

It only lasted for perhaps ten seconds, but while the two girls stared, stunned, at each other, it felt to Judy like a lifetime. Her head was spinning; she just couldn't think what to do. It was as though she was looking down at the scene in a dream, and she couldn't move.

Suzanne suddenly stepped forward, startling Judy, before turning sharply away to flee round the corner towards the main road. Judy stared at the retreating back of her sister. She shuddered, taking several long, deep breaths, wondering why she felt so relieved. She'd been searching for her twin for so long, and she knew she longed to meet her. She just had to speak to her. If she didn't do it now, she may never find her again.

"I've got to do it!" she muttered. And she took off after Suzanne.

The traffic was dense in the Edgware Road, and

there were people everywhere, blocking Judy's view of the pavement. Which way was she heading? If she jumps into a taxi, I'll never find her again. Then she spotted her. She was standing by the bus stop in front of Park West, trying to hail a cab.

She was wearing an expensive-looking, grey suit and carrying a black bag. As Judy rushed towards her, she turned, her hazel green eyes flashing towards Judy.

"Su!" yelled Judy, her arms held out towards her twin. She was only aware of her sister's anguished face, as she fought her way through the crowds towards her. She didn't hear the heavy running footsteps behind her.

Judy felt a hand on her shoulder and turned, startled, as a heavily-built man galloped past her, but when she looked back towards the bus stop, she couldn't see Suzanne anymore amongst the throng of people. As she walked quickly on, a loud screech of brakes and blaring car horns suddenly rent the air.

"What's happened?" she heard someone ask.

"Some idiot's hit the back of the bus," said a man.

Judy had almost reached the bus stop where Suzanne had been standing, but she wasn't there.

"Oh Su, where are you?" she murmured, starting to panic that she may have got away in a cab. Then she heard someone scream.

"Su?" she called loudly, her eyes darting over the faces around her. Reaching the edge of the kerb, she saw the man who had pushed past her. He was kneeling in the road in front of the bus with another man.

As if in a dream, Judy felt her legs walking towards them. The burly man looked up at her as she approached. They were pulling a jacket over something in the road. Judy stared down, unseeing.

"Su?" she muttered. "Suzanne?"

The man shook his head slowly, then standing up, placed his arm around Judy's shoulders and led her away.

CHAPTER TWENTY-TWO

Several weeks went by before Judy felt able to talk to Bob about Suzanne, and several more before Bob managed to convince her that she wasn't responsible for her sister's death. Judy had wept for days, certain that it was her fault; that if she hadn't been running after her, Suzanne would still be alive. But Bob had pointed out to her that Suzanne must have spotted the two policemen following Judy, and had run, either in a blind panic, or deliberately in front of the bus. The driver was in no way to blame, and was absolved of all responsibility.

The police had treated Judy kindly after the collision in the Edgware Road, and in particular, Inspector McGregor allowed Judy the time to recover from her shock before interviewing her.

Bob and Judy had moved into their new home, and were busy decorating when the phone rang one morning in mid-August.

"Who was it, darling?" called Judy, from the top of the ladder, where she was painting the dining room wall. Bob walked slowly into the room.

"I'm sorry, Judy," he said, "it was Chief Inspector McGregor, and he asked if you would call in at his office tomorrow."

"Oh no!" moaned Judy. "I can't. I'm too busy. What does he want?"

"I expect he wants to talk to you about Suzanne," said Bob.

"Well, I don't want to talk about her," snapped Judy, wiping her paintbrush backwards and forwards over the wall. "I want to forget her, you know I do!"

"Yes Judy, I know, but the Inspector has been very decent to wait so long, and you know you have nothing to fear from the police. He probably wants to let you know what they have found out about her."

"But I don't want to know about her, or what she may have done! Please darling, can't you tell him I'm ill or something?"

"If you will get down from that ladder, Judy, we can discuss this calmly," said Bob.

"All right, darling. I'm sorry," said Judy. "I just don't think I can face thinking about all that again," she said, as she clambered down the ladder clutching a swinging pot of paint in one hand.

By the following morning, Bob had managed to convince Judy that, for her own peace of mind, she needed to know the truth about her twin. That she would surely find it easier to forget Suzanne, if she knew more about her past, and whatever terrible things she may have done, rather than bravely continuing to convince herself that she had forgotten her, while all the time doubts and questions spun round in her head.

Bob took Judy's hand as they walked into the West End Police Station some five minutes early for their appointment with Chief Inspector McGregor.

Judy had spent the morning in town shopping, and had met Pat for a quick lunch.

"How was your morning, gorgeous?" asked Bob, as they sat down to wait.

"Super! I found some lovely things for the nursery," she replied.

Bob turned towards her, startled. "The nursery? You're not telling me…?"

Judy laughed. "No, darling, not yet! But we are going to have children, aren't we, so I may as well make a start on the spare bedroom."

"You are talking about a room for my son and heir, I take it," said Bob.

"No, for my beautiful daughter, of course!" joked Judy.

"Oh Lord, does that mean the house is going to be filled with fluffy pink rabbits?"

"Of course not!"

"Well, that's a relief. And how was Pat?" asked Bob, changing the subject.

"She's fine, but she was asking me if I had heard from Georgie, and I don't know whether I should tell the inspector about her, darling."

"Is that Suzanne's friend from New York?"

"Yes. Suzanne was staying at her flat, and Georgie wanted to help her to get away from London. She bought her a train ticket to Scotland."

"Well, that makes her an accomplice, doesn't it?" he remarked.

"But she wasn't to blame for what Suzanne did, was she? She just wanted to help her friend."

"Nonetheless, that still makes her guilty in the eyes of the law. Have the police asked you about her?"

"Oh no; they probably don't know of her existence."

"Then you should leave it that way, Judy. Suzanne's

gone now so there's no need for them to know about Georgie."

"I'm glad you've said that, darling. I wasn't sure what I should do. I won't mention her," said Judy, as Chief Inspector McGregor walked in to welcome them.

Having apologised for her seemingly uncooperative attitude during his investigation, Judy then asked Chief Inspector McGregor if he had anything to tell her about her twin.

"Yes, I do have quite a lot of information to pass on to you, Miss Hay," he replied. "We have put together quite a bulky file on Suzanne Greenberg, but firstly I wonder how much you know about the investigation into the illegal adoption racket and the babies stolen in 1952?"

"I don't really know very much," said Judy, "although I had intended to look in the newspapers archives to see if I could find out where the babies were taken. I thought it might have been mentioned in the court report of the nurse's trial."

"I'm afraid it wasn't," said McGregor. "But I can tell you that two of the babies sold to American couples did come from the Winchester Hospital."

"So Suzanne was one of them," said Judy.

"It would seem so, Miss Hay, but there is no way of proving it."

"But I know that the nurse who went to prison was there when we were born."

"Then you have your answer. Now, to get back to Suzanne Greenberg, Miss Hay: what I have to tell you is not pleasant, and you may find it upsetting."

"Are you sure you really want to hear this, Judy?" asked Bob.

"Yes darling, you said I should, and you're right,"

she replied. "I'm ready, Inspector." Judy then learned of the horrifying extent of her twin sister's psychosis.

Following Suzanne's death, the police forensic laboratory had sent blood samples to the Illinois CID, who immediately confirmed a match with not only the blood found at the scene of the Chicago crime, but also with the victim's missing wife's blood group. The New York Police had pieced together the story of Suzanne's tempestuous behaviour with the man later murdered in London; and the Massachusetts Police had reopened the files on the unsolved car crash which had killed Suzanne's parents. The car's brakes had been tampered with, but although staff at the house were convinced of her involvement, the original investigation had been unable to find any connection with the precocious ten-year-old child, despite strong psychological pointers.

It seemed evident, although unproven, that Suzanne Greenberg had killed four people.

EPILOGUE

It was a warm, dry December, and Bob and Judy had spent Saturday afternoon tidying up in the orchard behind the house. As Bob finished pruning the box hedge which separated the orchard from the garden, he glanced over as Judy reached up with the secateurs to cut a dead branch from one of the old apple trees.

"Be careful, gorgeous!" he called.

"Oh stop fussing, darling! I'm fine," she replied, as he hurried across to place a protective hand over the rounded bump under her heavy sweater. "I've never felt so fit and happy in all my life!"

"You are positively radiant, Judy, and I couldn't be happier. You really have forgotten all about her, haven't you?"

"Who?" she whispered.

"Suzanne."

"I don't know any Suzanne," said Judy, turning suddenly to press her lips hard against his in a loud kiss.

"Well done, gorgeous! Let's pack up and go inside for tea."

Bob turned to kiss her as they walked arm in arm into the house.

"I'm so happy!" he murmured, glancing up at the

setting sun. "And it'll be another lovely day tomorrow."

"And tomorrow, and tomorrow, and tomorrow..." whispered Judy.